D0593639

DESIGNS OF THE NIGHT SKY

NATIVE STORIERS: *A Series of American Narratives*
Series Editors: Gerald Vizenor, Diane Glancy

DESIGNS OF THE NIGHT SKY

Diane Glancy

University of Nebraska Press, Lincoln and London

 Manufactured in the United States of America. ⊗ Library of Congress Cataloging-in-Publication Data. Glancy, Diane. Designs of the night sky / Diane Glancy. p. cm. – (Native storiers) ISBN 0-8032-2190-8 (cloth : alk. paper) 1. Women storytellers – Fiction. 2. Women librarians – Fiction. 3. Cherokee women – Fiction. 4. Storytelling – Fiction. 5. Oklahoma – Fiction. I. Title. II. Series. PS3557.L294 D47 2002 813′.54 – dc21 2002017976

To native students at
Northeastern State
University in Tahlequah,
Oklahoma, and in
colleges everywhere.

CONTENTS

PREFACE

Designs of the Night Sky is a search for the meaning of written language in a Native American culture based on a history of oral tradition. In other words, how can writing take on the significance that the spoken language has had?

In *Designs of the Night Sky,* Ada Ronner and her husband are a librarian and a physics professor at Northeastern State University in Tahlequah, Oklahoma. Next to her husband, her two daughters, her large family, and her job in Manuscripts and Rare Books, Ada loves roller skating. Sometimes she loves it more than the library. Maybe because she hears the old stories in the sound of the skates. She hears the spoken word telling her the written word has to be. *Things change. Get used to it.*

Designs of the Night Sky takes place in the shape of small, titled chapters. Or named spaces. In *Artistry of Native American Myths* (University of Nebraska Press, 1998, page 154), Karl Kroeber says, "Indian myths are often constituted of distinct narrative units that may be told separately or in differing combinations." This "modular form," or "narrative modularity," as Kroeber calls it, became evident in the writing of *Designs of the Night Sky.*

The novel is a weaving of contemporary voices with several old texts, such as the historical journal of the Cherokee Removal from the Southeast to Indian Territory (present Oklahoma) (the Removal trail by river, not land).

The story is a mix of events moving between the turbulent history of a tribe and the survivors of that history still caught in turmoil. The reason, in Ada Ronner's voice, in the section called *The Sky Blowing with Stars: I believe in truth, which would become possible truth, which would become the possibilities of truth, which would become the truth of possibilities. Anything to shift the truth from what it is. The history of loss and silence about the loss. I want to open the shiftings, driftings. I want to fragment the solid block of it.*

ACKNOWLEDGMENTS

I am indebted to the following:

Singing of the Earth: A Native American Anthology, edited by Joseph Bruchac and Diana Landau, Walking Stick Press, San Francisco, 1993, for excerpts from "Whaling."

The Night Has a Naked Soul: Witchcraft and Sorcery among the Western Cherokee, Alan Kilpatrick, Syracuse University Press, 1997, for excerpts from various spells.

Acts of the Christian Martyrs, Herbert Musurillo, Oxford Press, 1972, for ideas from the story of Polycarp.

Poor Sarah or Religion Exemplified in the Life and Death of an Indian Woman, Elias Boudinot, the Manuscript and Archives Collection, University of Texas, Austin.

Artistry in Native American Myths, Karl Kroeber, University of Nebraska Press, 1998, for historical information in general and, in particular, *Bear Man, Aeonian,* translated from Cherokee.

Myths of the Cherokees, James Mooney, Annual Report of the Bureau of American Ethnology, no. 19 (Washington DC 1908), 327–29.

Cherokee Observer, Tahlequah, Oklahoma.

Xcp8 for excerpts from "Juan Gris / le livre," Kazim Ali.

Cherokee Stories, Reverend Watt Spade and Willard Walker, Carnegie

Corporation, Cross Cultural Educational Project of the University of Chicago, publication by the Laboratories of Anthropology, Wesleyan University, Middletown, Connecticut, 1966, for excerpts from "Relocation."

"Nootka and Quileute Music," Frances Densmore, Bureau of American Ethnology, bull. 124 (Washington DC 1939), for a whaling song.

"The Library" appeared on pages 4 to 14 in *A Loose Net of Words,* an anthology of poetry and creative prose by the winners of the McKnight Artist Fellowships for Writers, administered by The Loft.

Acknowledgment to a Wallace Faculty Travel Grant, Macalester College.

Acknowledgment also to *Physics: The Fabric of Reality,* Custom Academic Publishing Company, Oklahoma City, 1995, and to Contemporary Concepts, Physics II, taught by Professor Sung Kyu Kim at Macalester College, where I listened to my book as Kim lectured.

Acknowledgment to Elliott Bay Bookstore, Seattle, for the first reading from the manuscript on 20 November 1998.

Acknowledgment to Bread Loaf School of English–New Mexico campus, where a part of the manuscript was read during the commencement address on 5 August 1999.

Acknowledgment to a reading at Woodland Pattern Bookstore in Milwaukee, Wisconsin, on 4 December 1999, and for publication of the broadside "Creation Myths for the Written Word."

Acknowledgment to the *Cream City Review,* vol. 24, no. 2 (fall 2000), 66, for publication of "The Dust Bowl (2)."

Thanks to Dolores Sumner, Manuscript and Rare Book Librarian, Northeastern State University, Tahlequah, Oklahoma. Thanks also to Cat McCormick, who opened the Manuscript and Rare Book Room for me one Saturday when it was closed so I could find a reference.

Thanks to Murv Jacob for "We Take Our Designs from the Night Sky."

DESIGNS OF THE NIGHT SKY

Christian Indians make me laugh.

Jack Malotte

something stone to use
provider above to rest, you
now you will tell me
what I am thinking about

"To Divine with the Stones" (old Cherokee spell),
The Night Has a Naked Soul, Alan Kilpatrick

The few books rescued from the ashes were burned on the sides, the corners rounded by fire. Almost learned to read the centers of the books and then he imagined the stories from the absence of the words, from the words that were burned.

Hotline Healers, Gerald Vizenor

Ecstasy reveals a round chamber containing a great book with a continuous back circling the walls of the room.

"The Library of Babel" *Ficciones,* Jorge Luis Borges

THE LIBRARY

The books have voices. I hear them in the library. In Manuscripts and Rare Books where I work. I know the voices are from the books. Yet I know the old stories do not like books. Do not like the written words. Do not like libraries. The old stories carry all the voices of those who have told them. When a story is spoken, all those voices are in the voice of the narrator. But writing the words of a story kills the voices that gather in the sound of the storytelling. The story is singular then. Only one voice travels in the written words. One voice is not enough to tell a story. Yet I can hear a voice telling its story in the archives of the university library. I hear the books. Not with my ears, but in my imagination. Maybe the voices camp in the library because the written words hold them there. Maybe they are captives with no place else to go.

GREASY GRAVY

Where are the old days? Not the old days of the Removal, but the old days I remember. What was there? My grandmother's greasy gravy. A barn. My grandfather. The stock. My mother's family name, Adair, from which my name, Ada, was taken.

My father's '48 Ford looked black, but in the sun, it was the blackgreen of a bottlefly. The upholstery scratched as I sat between my three brothers. I was glad to get to my grandparents' house. In their yard, a night storm flashed lightning and wind that felled a tree, sweeping the roof with its leaves. I felt lost somewhere in the branches with the little people in the woods. When I looked from the window, I could see the blackgreen night greased with rain. In flashes of lightning, I saw my father's car underneath one of the large limbs that had fallen. In another flash I saw my father in the drive holding a jacket over his head. Sometimes I feel I was in that car when the tree hit. In the years of trouble that followed, I felt my brothers were in the car too.

My family took the bus back from Sallisaw to Tahlequah (Oklahoma). I remember thinking of the two trails of our people during Removal. Had my grandfather talked about them again? Overland and by water.

But then, on that trip, it had been by bus.

The farm, the barn, the animals. All had seemed small. A tree could fall across them, hide them underneath its limbs. Smaller. Smallest. Like the voices stuffed into a story. Like the history of a nation in a book.

The flashes of lightning were a camera taking pictures. The images of the storm, the tree, are an album in my head. My brothers, Robert, Wayne, and Raymond, crowding the window. I still can see their faces as if I'd been outside with my father looking up at them.

Maybe written words are a photograph of the voice. Maybe there always will be dissatisfaction. Didn't my mother complain of the photographs of herself in the family album? Wasn't I dissatisfied with mine also?

PARAGRAPHS

You won't like them, but you will get used to them. You will come to recognize the way they work. The squares of writing called paragraphs. The squares as houses in a neighborhood (which a book is).

Once, the words were going everywhere. The words didn't know how to be written. Imagine them rolling all over the pages.

Imagine writing without paragraphs.

The paragraphs are a place for the words to stay. One thought after another kept on track.

Words are the furniture of the paragraph.

Reading opens the windows.

A paragraph is a box written in. On.

A field.

A nest.

(A paragraph is seen on the page, but is it an object?)

Once, the voice got tired of being sound. It wanted to be seen. It didn't know writing was the Removal trail of the voice.

At one time, the voice was a tall tree. But there was a storm.

Words open like an umbrella. You read and there is a (roof) covering you.

I talk to Riley as we walk through the leaves. My oldest brother, Robert, drops Riley, his daughter, at my house. He doesn't want her riding with the boy she likes. I walk her to school on my way to the library at Northeastern State. I tell her about words as we walk. Sometimes we hear the past in our feet through the leaves.

THERE WERE THE OLD DAYS OF THE INDIAN REMOVAL

EMIGRATING TO THE WEST BY BOAT

(Original in the National Archives Office of Indian Affairs, Washington DC, *"Cherokee Emigration" C–553 "Special File 249.")*

IN THE ROUTE OF EMMIGRATION OF A PARTY OF CHEROKEE INDIANS, KEPT BY LIEUT. EDWD DEAS, U.S. ARMY, CONDUCTOR OF THE PARTY, FROM WATERLOO, ALABAMA TO THE NEW COUNTRY WEST OF THE MISSISSIPPI RIVER.

6th April 1838

Yesterday a Party of Cherokee Indians, in number Two hundred & fifty, together with some other emigrants of the same tribe who are removing on their own resources, arrived near Waterloo, Ala. by water, under charge of the Superintendent of the Cherokee Emigration. The S. Boat *Smelter,* provided under the contract for Transportation, had been waiting the arrival of the Party, and today the Indians were established on board of this boat, one large Keel with double cabins, made & furnished in the manner mentioned in the contract.

The Present Party having been previously Enrolled, were today turned over to me as Conductor and immediately afterwards (about 10 O'Clock

A.M.) the boat was got under weigh and continued to run until after sunset, having come more than 100 miles and laid by on account of the darkening of night.

The *Smelter* appears to be a very good boat, over 150 Tuns Burthen, a fast vessel, and well adapted to the business of removal of Indians. The Keel in tow is commodious and appears convenient for the Indians. Temporary cooking-hearths are constructed on the top of it, and there is a cooking stove in the after part of the Steam Boat.

A CALL

A library is a place for keeping words in their books. At one time, stories were kept in memory. The invisible library from which libraries come. A storyteller had stories that sometimes lasted seven days (or seven years), using beads or stones for reminders where the voice went during a story.

Barrels of cheap pork.

Boats over water (stopping once to wood).

The party is to have the entire use of the keel boat, and all parts of the steamboat but the cabins.

A neighborhood of houses on wheels. A skating rink.

When the story lives, the paragraphs seem to move as skaters on the roller rink.

A paragraph is a state of grace.

A story is a subdivision in the suburbs.

A written composition that consists of one or more sentences, deals with one point or gives the words of one speaker, and begins on a new indented line.

Some read in the boats called books. Reading is *oaring.* Is moving the story upriver.

My brother Wayne calls me at work and says to feed his kids. *He was,* he said, what was it?

ENCAMPMENT

Outside the library, the leaves are falling. I think they sound like pages turning as I walk through them. It is sound that carries the story, not the particular words. No. It *was* sound that carried the story.

Inside the library, a young man climbs the stairs to Manuscripts and Rare Books. He is looking for a master's thesis on Cherokee ceremony.

YOUNG MAN: "I wanted to know if I was doing the stomp dance the way it'd been done. I asked an elder, he said, oh, it's written down in that library over there."

I take the young man to the theses section.

Are the books content in their encampment in the library? They are cataloged and in their place, yet they circulate. I like to think of them as camps lined up on the hills. One camp can hear others on the shelves. But why are they murmuring, more now than before?

I think of my brothers and their families in their disrupted lives. But Cherokee history is turbulent. There's always been rumblings and uprisings and disagreements. When I open the *Cherokee Observer,* I'm afraid I'll see my brothers' names. Robert Nonoter arrested after a fistfight at the Dust Bowl over tribal politics. Wayne Nonoter arrested, assaulting his wife. Raymond is the only one who usually escapes notice. But he is full of his own hostilities, griefs, and angers. He just doesn't release them. It probably has been two years since he was arrested for brawling. But Robert is taking up the slack. His children following. Who knows how far they will go?

I'm preoccupied as I walk through the leaves to the house where my daughters, Noel and Nolie, are cooking supper. Wes Stand, Noel's boyfriend, sits with Wayne's children as they watch television. My husband is in his chair reading the newspaper. I sit on his lap, crumpling the paper beneath me. I would stay longer, but Nolie calls me from the kitchen.

NOLIE: "Uncle Wayne left Clare, Stu, and Grace and told us not to tell Aunt Cora where they were."

ADA: "She'll know where they are. Where else do they leave their children? Has Cora called?"

NOLIE: "No."

ADA: "Where're the girls?"

NOEL: "In our room."

ADA: "Your old dolls don't get a rest."

NOLIE: "Clare and Grace just like to be in our room."

I think of Wayne with Cora, his wife, after him. At least they'll have a night to fight without the children hearing them.

At least my mother won't call saying the spirits that guard the children are keeping her awake.

But more than Wayne, it's Robert. My oldest brother, Robert.

THE DUST BOWL (1)

At the Dust Bowl, Tahlequah's roller rink, my skates are the wheels of a plane. I feel them under me. Where do I go when I take off? The wooded hills and rolling land of northeastern Oklahoma. The post oaks and black-jacks, the corner posts in fields. When I skate at the rink, I am the written word let loose in spoken story. I hear the other voices with which mine can be known. Other voices by which mine will not be alone.

I've known Ether, my husband, since grade school. Our mailbox says *Charles John Ronner,* but he's been called Ether since high school when he put himself to sleep in physics. Ether Ronner is the dirt field from which I take off in my crop duster.

The Dust Bowl was where the wind pulled up tree roots, fence posts, the land itself blew north. I still feel the updraft, uplift, updrift of the wind in my ears. I skate in a whirlwind. Ether is the strength of dust. He is the substance of the land. But I have to have air. The space above the fields of the library where I work.

Ether limits me to four hours at the roller rink on Saturdays. I put on my skates and leave him behind. He never could keep up. All he can do is float through the dust cloud I leave as I take off. Sometimes I hold out my arms. Ada Ronner. I cover ground. Under my rolling feet. My first roller skates were metal frames with wheels I strapped to my shoes. I skated awkwardly over the uneven walks where an old tree had lifted a slab of the walk and I had to jump or else trip. I had walk-skated more than skated, not really rolling anywhere.

My story is the eight small wheels under my feet in the roller rink. A circle within a square, though the building is more of a rectangle, and the rink more of an oval. The roller rink is a trickster hiding its magic, its floor of maple strips, waxed, polished, waiting. I hear the sound of wheels on the floor as I lace the skates on my feet. I hear the old Cherokee voices as I skate. They're from the library also. Maybe Manuscripts and Rare Books is a skating rink for the spirit world. I know the voices talk while they skate. I know I skate with the ancestors. Once they get going.

I look for Robert, my brother, as I skate. He's a truck driver. He can't stop the momentum when he gets back from a long haul. He can't come in off the road. The highway goes on, pulling his truck along with it. He can't sleep, can't sit still in his house. His wife and children are afraid because he looks for a fight to release his tension. I bring him to the rink. Slow him down on skates.

ADA: "When I skate, I feel like you do when you drive."

ROBERT: "You don't come close."

ADA: "There's a release."

ROBERT: "You go in circles."

ADA: "Do you remember how we sat on the roof of the pig pen on Grandpa's farm?"

ROBERT: "I remember Grandpa after me with his switch."

ADA: "The sow would have hurt you."

ROBERT: "He could have told me to stay out."

ADA: "I think he did. I remembered to stay out of the pen."

ROBERT: "Too bad we all can't be like you."

ADA: "Feel the wind as you skate, Robert. It's like turning into heaven."

ROBERT: "Not anywhere near. Heaven is out on the road when you're high on driving and your dreams stomp dance in your head."

ADA: "Why don't you pull off and sleep?"
ROBERT: (he wants to leave) "I got a timeline to meet."
ADA: "Just keep skating."
ROBERT: "You're offering me a rink when I need a Roller Derby. A toy truck when I'm used to eighteen wheels."
ADA: "What do you dream, Robert?"
ROBERT: "The road keeps going and never stops."

BEFORE

Sometimes the voices talk about the old march. From 1820 to 1840, there were several overland trails from the Southeast to Indian Territory, which later became Oklahoma. There were several marches over several years on those trails. But there also had been removal by river. From the Hiwassee in North Carolina, to the Tennessee River, to the Ohio, to the Mississippi, to the Arkansas. *Oars,* I think when I hear the voices. Rowing over river routes at various times in various groups. Flatboats and steamboats without oars.

Maybe Robert is still bound up in the old travel of the tribe. A spirit stuck to him, steaming in the night air. Sometimes I think I feel that spirit. Maybe from the Removal trail. I'm sure I've seen steam rise from Robert when he steps from his rig.

7TH APRIL, 1838

The Boats got under weigh this morning at eight and continued to run without any occurrence of importance until near sunset, when we reached Paducah at the mouth of Tennessee River, and anchored a short time near the Town, not willing to land on account of the Indians having access to the Whiskey shops. On attempting to set out again about dark, some water washed into the Keel, (owing to the waves in the Ohio) and the Indians were seized with fear ——— rushed out of it into the steamboat.

There was no danger, but I found it would be impossible to *convenice* them of that and therefore determined to proceed without the Keel, the S. Boat being large enough to transport the party by giving them the main cabin and lower and forward decks, and having cooking hearths constructed on them later.

The Party having been removed to the S. Boat, we set out from the mouth of Tennessee River about 10 P.M. and are now progressing rapidly toward the mouth of the Ohio.

THE SEVEN CLANS OF THE CHEROKEE NATION

The Messengers	Bird Clan
The Builders	Blue Clan
The Clothes Makers	Deer Clan
The Teachers and Priests	Longhair Clan
The Medicine Men	Paint Clan
Ballplayers and Gamekeepers	Wild Potato Clan
The Warriors and Protectors	Wolf Clan

THE DREAM (1)

I hear them all. Could imagine them if I didn't. The spirits. The Little People. Over there. On the ridge. They come after dark. I hear them revving their motors on the hill. Their old cars. Fords and Chevys of the spirits. I hear them in the updraft of pines. I see Robert in his rig. The long line of trucks on a vertical road from the earth. The stars as headlights. The spirit warriors with beaded eyes riding on the hood. Trucks ascending and descending on Jacob's ladder (Genesis 28:12). The whole road trembles as if a small helicopter lands with those silent wings that turn on its head. Later the spirits get out their tambourines. They sing their songs to the Maker. The ordinator of the universe. Orator of the world that is both seen and unseen.

Their voices come from dreams.

Who are we to speak?

What have we got to say when there are no answers?

How do we pry the sun out of the ground when it comes up anyway in another place than where we ask?

What do we do in the shadow world?

How do we come back from the edge of the earth?

One spirit is back from an ancient gathering on the northern plains. There's a green spirit with antlers on his head. A yellow spirit who trembles like a stalk of corn. They are a ghostly tribe staying up too late, remembering the Removal trail, the lost years that followed, the boarding school, all weighted with despair.

I hear thunder in my dream. There is lightning from the edge of the hill that is a crooked streak backfiring from Albert Antelope's car.

Why am I a receiver of the voices? A receptor? I might as well stand in an open field with metal curlers during a storm.

Sometimes I dream of the Baptist Church on Sunday. I live in a world neither Jesus, nor the spirits, nor the Little People can fill, but they overlap in places.

I don't like the hymns that tell my voice what to do. I can't read the notes anyway. But when we praise the Maker in church, my voice goes where it wants.

JESUS

We go to church on Sunday. Noel and Nolie are downstairs for their Sunday school class, then they join us for church. Sometimes they sit with their friends.

Jesus, I have given you what you are wishing to get – nails driven by a hammer. And now you have them. Hold them with your strong hands and feet and do not let them go. Jesus, look at us and you will see us come to see you. We will say to one another: "What a great Savior he is! What a holy Savior!" And you, Jesus, will be proud of all that you will hear us say of your greatness. Jesus, do not turn to the sky, but hug the land, for we will cover your body with bluebill duck feathers and the down of an eagle, the chief of all birds; for this is what you are wishing, and this is what you are trying to find from one end of the world to the other.

LIFTED

The flock of birds lifts from the field as I pass. Stu watches them as I drive him back to Wayne's. The girls, Clare and Grace, decided to stay with my girls. The birds sound like rustling silk. Mary Nonoter, my mother, feeds the birds. She says she has visions of Indian people in the afterlife, speckled as starlings with spots of light. A whole flock. Across the hills, the gray clouds hang like the net of them flying. The birds could be holes. The spaces between the birds are air. The birds rise as words from one field landing in another. Maybe they are on their way south.

See the horse with mud clomped on his hoofs? His hair matted with rain. Sometimes it rains in clumps. The days are gray for nearly a week. A hurricane on its way north, blowing out as it goes.

There is the land and the sky. Hills and trees. Fields scattered with houses and a barn now and then. A road through them. Somewhere, the Arkansas River that brought some of the ancestors on boats from the original territory in the Southeast. Not the ones that walked, but those who *rowed* the boats.

The spoken words are eating the corn, cooking potatoes. I hear one of the voices telling a story as I drive:

Sound thought it existed all alone. Sound spoke the sky and the land into being because it could shape. If sound kept on with its sound, it always would be all that is. But something else began to be made. Because sound had space, could shape it, could also have shape. Sound made itself into words that could be seen. Words became themselves with themselves. They became rain on the barn. They became the stock in the barn. They became something with shape that could be seen. What is the library but a barn? What are written words but the voice tamed? Domesticated. The written words are animals in their pastures. Fenced. It has to be. Sound has a different way to be recognized. The voice still will be there. It isn't going away. The voice always will be the voice, but now it has another way to say. Sound can be written words. A flock or herd of them. The written words come in books. Shelves hold them. The library is a reminder the written words are stuck in this world. They will not go to the other world the voice alone can transcend.

THE NESTS OF BOATS

Manuscripts and Rare Books is in an upstairs corner of the university library. There's an anteroom with the card catalog and librarian's desk, a few cases of Cherokee artifacts, and the cabinet of map drawers. A mural of Cherokee history on the wall. Then there's the large room with a row of windows up near the ceiling. And the shelves of books.

A wire enclosure something like a chicken coop is in a corner of Manuscripts and Rare Books where old books in boxes, genealogies and archives, Cherokee testaments, Cherokee primers, books of magic and old spells, and other rare books, such as *Poor Sarah* and *Relocation,* are shelved.

What should I ask the voices? Why do I hear their murmurings more often now?

In the afternoon, the sky brings in its wet sacks. It is cold and damp. The heat has not been turned on yet. What I want is climate control for the Cherokee books and documents. The ceiling is high. I keep fans running in the corners to circulate air. Once in a while, an official from the Oklahoma Historical Society comes and listens, but nothing is ever done. No thermostat for Manuscripts and Rare Books. In winter, when the heat is on, it rises from the floor below. By May I want to claw out the windows.

It's when I feel the Removal trail by river. Up the Tennessee, the Ohio, the Mississippi, the Arkansas. The nests of boats floating there. The sun coming in as if a window above them.

Someone leaves a *New York Times* on a bench in the anteroom. I see a caption: *Egypt Carvings Set Earlier Date for Alphabet* (John Noble Wilford, Sunday, November 14, 1999). I sit down and read the article:

On the track of an ancient road in the desert west of the Nile – some inscriptions on limestone – earliest known examples of alphabetic writing. The Semitic script with Egyptian influences – dated to somewhere between 1900–1800 B.C., two to three centuries earlier than previously recognized uses of a nascent alphabet.

The alphabet – an invention by workaday people – democratized writing. Alphabetic writing emerged as a shorthand by which fewer than 30 symbols, each one representing a single sound, could be combined to form words for a wide variety of things – and ideas.

The written word left a record. It happened to the Cherokees in 1821 when Sequoyah invented the syllabary. It made an illiterate people literate.

But they still did not write about the Removal trail. That record was left by white lieutenants.

But if it were not for the written word, there would be only a few, floating voices.

Otherwise the journey would be lost.

A NEW SACRED GROUND

When I skate, I can stand on the ridge south of Tahlequah and see the valleys below. What is beyond them? Do I have an atlas? Do I know the old sacred grounds? Where have I gone other than the migrations around the Dust Bowl? Why would I want anywhere else to go? I have a large family:

Rabah, my sister-in-law, married to my oldest brother, Robert, who stews in the heat of the highway, calls: Could I watch their children, Riley and George?

Cora, my sister-in-law, married to Wayne, my middle brother, who doesn't always come home at night, calls: Could I watch their children, Grace, Clare, and Stu?

Shuba, my sister-in-law, married to Raymond, my youngest brother, who is what ______ I hear? (Campaigning for a witch?) Shuba asks: Could I take care of the three boys? Noah, Tubal, and Caleb?

All of them like *tar babies* I can't get my hands back from.

The voices tell stories in the roller rink. *Family is your most important possession.* (Or do I think it's words?)

ETHER: "But you don't get anywhere in the roller rink."

ADA: "That's what Robert said. But you travel to the point of departure."

ETHER: "Again and again?"

It's written in the sound of my skates. It's the sound of the voice that is the topsoil, lifted up and blown away, turning the sky black with words from their pages.

THE STARS AS ROLLER RINKS

While Ether was putting himself to sleep in high school, I wrote a report on roller skating.

Wheeled skates were used in Holland in the eighteenth century, but it was the invention of the four-wheeled skate by J. L. Plimpton in New York in 1863.

Later, the Raymond skate with ball and cone bearing.

The first wheels were made of boxwood, but the wearing of their edges.

Because the ice melted and they wanted to keep going.

I make a creation story. One night, a small comet fell to the earth, leaving a round rink in the ground. Because the stars, the planets, the moons, with their roller skates on. Is why they move around the rink of the sky. I skate with the planets in their orbits around the blackgreen air of the universe.

I name the wheels of my skates.

East. South. West. North.

East. North. West. South.

The Vikings skated on cow ribs or the bones of horses or reindeer, bound to the feet with thongs.

The earliest dated skate was found in Björkö, Sweden, between the eighth and tenth centuries. Bone skates also were found in Norway, Denmark, the Netherlands, England, Germany, Switzerland. I imagine the idea carried on boats across the Atlantic.

The Dutch word, *schaats,* dated from 1573. The word was found in Hexham's 1648 *Dictionarie.*

There was a Scandinavian saga, *Fornmanna Sogur,* 1320.

Samuel Pepys in his 1 December 1662 entry, "people sliding with the Skeats."

John Evelyn in his entry of the same date told of the sliders on the new canal in St. James's Parke. "How swiftly they pass, how suddenly they stop."

I move on the rink in the Dust Bowl. In the old days I could (skate the patterns) *ball of twine, rail fence, straight and curved cut Maltese crosses, hook star, pig's ear star, heel pivot star, Tahlequah grapevine.* While my brothers jumped the ramp of the uneven sidewalk with their bicycles. While they skidded over the gravel roads in their trucks.

The rink is full of Ether's physics. I can feel the four forces as I skate. Gravity. Electromagnetism. The stronger and weaker forces. Ether out of bounds at my discontinuous leaps. My quantum skating.

WHALING

Whale, I have given you what you are wishing to get – my good harpoon. And now you have it. Hold it with your strong hands and do not let go. Whale, turn toward the beach and you will see the young men come down from my village to see you; and the young men will say to one another: "What a great whale he is! What a fat whale he is!" And you, whale, will be proud of all that you will hear them say. Do not turn outward, but hug the shore, for when you come ashore, young men will cover your great body with bluebill duck feathers and with the down of the great eagle, the chief of all birds; for this is what you are wishing, and this is what you are trying to find from one end of the world to the other.

ARRIVAL

I became a Christian because they teach forgiveness.
In the old Indian way, no one forgave anything.
Agnes Pumpkin

I walk up the hill from school. Before I turn the corner onto Summit, I hear Raymond's boys, Noah, Tubal, and Caleb (I want to call him Cain) yelling in the yard. Wes's art car covered with fishing lures and a small outboard motor is parked at the curb. Where are Noel and Nolie, my girls? They're supposed to be watching their cousins.

I never know where the boys are headed or what's going to be left after they've gone. Tubal is chasing Noah with a stick as long as he is. They have torn down some of the woodpile crawling over it. The neighbor's dog is barking. I call to the boys (my nephews) to stop fighting. They run past me through the yard.

ADA: "Where's your father? That tribal election can't be over soon enough. Where's Shuba? Conjuring her spells? Why am I the dumping ground for everyone's children?"

Inside, Nolie is in the kitchen making Rainy Mountain with her mashed potatoes. Wes and Ether have their feet on the low table in front of the sofa.

ADA: "Get those boys in here. Tie them to their chairs at the table."

ETHER: "I'll bring 'em in."

WES: "I can't stay."

NOLIE: "Eey yaw, Dad, go get 'em."

Wes drives off, the propeller on his outboard turning.

Ether ropes the boys in their chairs.

NOLIE: "Grandma called. She wants you to take her to the doctor."

ADA: "Has she forgotten I work? Has she forgotten what it's like to have children scattered all over the house?"

NOEL: "Wes and I will take her after school."

ADA: "I've got to go to the grocery too – for the cookout over there. My sisters-in-law could do some of the shopping."

THE PARENTS' HOUSE

We go to our parents' house.

THE PARENTS: Obed and Mary Nonoter.

The three brothers and their families:

Robert and Rabah, their children, Riley and George.

Wayne and Cora, Stu and the girls, Clare and Grace.

Raymond and Shuba, the boys, Noah, Tubal, and Caleb.

Sometimes the Stands, so they can see their son, Wes, as they say.

Sometimes Ether's parents. His sister.

Sometimes neighbors we've known since we were children.

Sometimes friends of the children.

Then, of course, Ether (Charles John Ronner) and Ada (me), our daughters, Noel and Nolie. (Noel is the reason Wes Stand is always at our house.)

We gather in my parents' backyard to cook. It's still warm. Sometimes the children, hot and sweaty after running in the yard, take off their sweaters. Then Rabah, Cora, and Shuba yell at the children to put their sweaters back on before they chill. My girls, Noel and Nolie, run after the children to corral them again.

Robert, Wayne, and Raymond huddle as if boys wanting to retreat into the backseat of the family car, as if remembering when they made their own way down the road without families and responsibility; when they were the responsibility our parents had. They are grouchy with their wives and children; they are at odds with the world in which they have to live, unable to catch up with whatever moves ahead of them, always behind, overwhelmed at every turn. They are angry and hurt; they flee to the wildlife refuge of their arguments. They claw at one another and play out their wars on themselves.

Maybe they are afraid of being husbands and fathers because it is a difficult instinct. It splays them between self and offspring. Which would survive? Could both? Maybe they didn't have enough of themselves to disperse to anyone. Why? Maybe it was growing up Cherokee in Cherokee County.

Ether turns the burgers. Why is he different from my brothers? What happened that made him want to have ideas in his head like constellations? Why are others left out? Robert thinking of the load he pulls in his truck; Wayne his construction work; Raymond, what job does he have now?

I hear the voices of Robert and Wayne. Robert has him in the ditch by the creek behind my parents' house. Cora yelling that Robert will break Wayne's neck.

Their voices are a tag team of crows in the trees, or starlings at dusk, or the locusts that come in seven-year plagues to deafen the evening with their noise. How they argue. Wild and helpless.

My father is there now, pulling apart two of his sons. Wes's father, Wes, and Ether are there; the neighbors coming now. I don't know where Raymond is. Robert must have had a few beers before he came. There's no drinking on my father's property. None. If they want to drink, they have to do it before they come.

The children are crying in fear of the men's violence, or they are fighting among themselves. Stu is the only one too young to understand, but this time even he seems to look with recognition.

But what is there to understand? The Cherokees are roily as if they just stepped off the boats after Removal, ready to kill those who signed the treaty. What has changed?

Shuba comforts my mother, who is crying.

My father pulls Robert and Wayne to the yard. He sits them in the lawn chairs and stands beside them. I see the veins stand out in his neck. How many times have my brothers wrecked our cookout? How many times have we eaten with anger stuffed in our throats?

ADA: "What if the children act like you?"

ROBERT: "You're the only one with a cowbell around your neck."

I'm not sure what he means, but Ether seems angry. I remind him of the burgers (charred) and he takes them off the grill.

My mother calls everyone to the table. Robert and Wayne stand up, their legs unstable as if they just got off the boat.

THE LIBRARIAN

I didn't want to be a librarian. I didn't know what else I wanted to do. Ether knew from the beginning he wanted to study physics. His mother hung stars over his crib; he reached for them since he was an infant. When Ether went to the University of Oklahoma for his Ph.D. in physics, I studied at Northeastern State University in Tahlequah and worked in the library and skated at the rink. Ether returned to Northeastern to teach because I didn't want to leave Tahlequah.

I kept working at the library, kept taking courses. Maybe the library is my city of refuge. (Among the cities, six shall be for a refuge (Christ) which you shall assign for the manslayer that he might flee there (Numbers 35:6).)

But if I was going to be a librarian, I didn't want to work in Manuscripts and Rare Books. I wanted to be in Acquisitions or Circulation or Reference or Periodicals, where I could be on the floor. Where I could see others. But I was put on the second floor in the archives where a student comes in and I have to make sure the book is handled properly, not permitted to leave the reading room, nor marked in. I assist those who do research and want the old voices. The stories of the Cherokee tribe were recorded by soldiers during the Removal, by ethnographers, by the WPA project. Some of the books are chants and old magic. Before they knew stories weren't to be written. Or early writers or early writings of other writers. Or early editions or whatever came under the heading of Manuscripts and Rare Books. Whatever could be gathered in Special Collections.

I begin to think the books want me here. They want me to hear what they say. They talk from the written word. Maybe writing doesn't kill the voice. Put it in a grave. Maybe writing isn't the destroyer people think it is.

Sometimes ethnographers wrote down the voices in their own way. The ethnographers didn't always get it right. Or if they did, the voices didn't want to be written. They try to get out of the writing as if it were a straight jacket or restraining order. Sometimes I know the murmurings I hear are the voices struggling to cover themselves; to get out of the books. But where would they go?

MORE OF THE OLD DAYS OF REMOVAL

I sit in Manuscripts and Rare Books. No one comes to ask for assistance. I open the papers of the Cherokee Emigration. I feel the oars in my hand.

9th April, 1838

We reached Memphis last night about 12 P.M. and stopped a short time to procure some Fresh Beef and other supplies. The Boat then continued to run (stopping once to wood) until about 3 o'clock this afternoon, when we reached Montgomery's Point and there stopped in the stream a short time to take in a Pilot for the Arkansas River. We then entered White River, passed thro' the cut-off, and are now ascending the Arkansas and are about 50 miles above *it's* mouth (9 o'clock P.M.). We find the Arkansas not very high, but shall probably be able to reach Little Rock and may perhaps go higher. The present party has been subsisting since starting on Bacon, Pork, Flour meal, and a small quantity of Fresh Beef.

10th April, 1838

We continued to run last night until about 11 o'clock when a slight accident happened to the machinery, the Boat was obliged to lie by 3 or 4 hours, and then set out again and continued to run (stopping once to wood) from that time until this evening about 7, and then stopped for the night, it being too dark, and the water too shallow to proceed until the morning. We are now 40 or 50 miles below Little Rock.

11th April, 1838

The Boat got under weigh this morning early and reached Lt. Rock about ½ past 11 A.M. I had her anchored in the stream to prevent access to Whiskey and went on shore for the purpose of consulting the Principal Disbursing Agent as to the probability of being able to proceed further up the river on *The Smelter.*

I found it would be useless to attempt to proceed further in a Boat of her size, and therefore made an arrangment with the S. Boat *Little Rock* which is, I found on the point of setting out for the upper Parts with two Keels in tow.

The Captain agreed to take the present Party as far up as possible for $5 each for the whole distance and proportionately for less, which I ascertained to be a reasonable term, and the best arrangement I could possibly make at present. The Party is to have the entire use of one Keel, the Top of the other, & all parts of the S. Boat except the cabins. After landing some provisions from *The Smelter* I proceeded with the Party on board of her, about 5 miles above the town and landed for the night.

I purchased to day under authority from the Superintendent of the Cherokee Emmigration, Eighty Barrels of (cheap?) Pork, and Eighty barrels of Flour, and turned them over to the Principal Mil. Disb. Agent at Little-rock, for the use of the Cherokee Emmigration in the ensuing summer & fall. I obtained this provision by paying only it's cost and carriage.

12th April, 1838

The Little Rock Keels are heavily loaded the other nearly empty and fitted up for the Indians ——— arrived last night at the point at which I stopped the Party, and early this morning the people and their Baggage were transfered from *The Smelter.* We then immediately got under weigh and proceeded 5 or 6 miles, when the heavy Keel sprung a leak from running on a Bar or Snag, whereupon the Captain found it necessary to run ashore to prevent her from sinking. The whole day has been consumed in getting out the Freight from this Keel and stopping the leak.

I have determined, if possible, to induce the Captain to leave his heavy Keel and all his freight, and take with all possible dispatch, as beside other reasons the Small-Pox is in this section of country, a disease, apparently of all other the most fatal to Indians.

14th April, 1838

The Indians were got on board this morning at light and the boats have continued to run thro' the day, only stopping a short time to Wood, and by 3 o'clock P.M. had come 50 miles and reached White's on Lewiston Bar 4 miles below that place. The Keel was then landed and every means ———.

15th April, 1838

This morning after the people had their breakfast, they walked about 5 miles up the south bank of the Arkansas for the purpose of lightening the Boat. A different channel was then tried by the Captain with success, and by noon we reached a second Bar about 2 miles above Lewiston.

16th April, 1838

The forenoon spent in trying to force the S. Boat over the Bar without effect, and the afternoon was consumed in getting her ashore on the north bank of the river.

17th April, 1838

Much rain fell last night and the people not having Tents, I found it necessary to hire a small house to protect them from the weather. This morning another trial was made to go over the Bar which was successful, and about 11 A.M. the S. boat reached the point which the Indians were encamped and after taking the Party on board continued to run until a short time after dark, and stopped for the night at the foot of Five Island, having come between 30 & 40 miles. Rations of Prime *Vork,* Fresh Beef & Flour were issued to day for 4 days as usual.

Edwd. Deas
Liet. U.S. Army
Conductor

AT THE IGUANA CAFÉ

My brother Raymond calls the police when Cora and Wayne fight. Raymond is afraid Wayne will hurt her.

WAYNE: "My own brother turns me in!"

ADA: "How do we know what you'll do when you rage?"

WAYNE: "He wants the heat off his back."

ADA: "We all live in Tahlequah, Wayne. Do you know what it's like to open the *Observer* and see your name?"

WAYNE: "Nonoter isn't your name anymore."

ADA: "I mean *your* name. What's the matter with you?"

WAYNE: "Maybe things don't go as well for the rest of us."

ADA: "I work at the library. Students come in to read the newspaper. They see your name."

WAYNE: "I'm sorry I embarrass you."

ADA: "It isn't only me. Noel and Nolie see it too. Robert and Raymond's children. You know we're all related."

WAYNE: "You aren't responsible for me."

ADA: "You leave Stu and the girls with Noel and Nolie. Stu can't read yet, but he knows."

WAYNE: "I pay your girls. Robert leaves his too."

ADA: "Raymond too. Why can't you get along with your wife?"

WAYNE: "Leave me alone, Ada. You sound just like her."

ADA: "Do you remember the old bus trip after the tree fell on our car?"

WAYNE: "No."

ADA: "We took the bus back to Tahlequah from Grandpa's?"

WAYNE: "I remember the bus."

ADA: "Why were we on it?"

WAYNE: "We didn't have a car."

ADA: "Why didn't we?"

WAYNE: "We didn't own one yet."

ADA: "Yes we did, Wayne. It was smashed in Grandpa's drive in a storm – I can see you and Robert and Raymond in the upstairs window."

WAYNE: "I told you I don't remember."

ADA: "We were on the same bus back to Tahlequah, Wayne. Still are. We changed seats so often, Dad finally told us to sit still. We're on the same bus, no matter what seat we're sitting in."

LATE

I hurry through the leaves to the library. I'm late. The trees surround me. I walk from Summit where we live on the hill above the campus, past the high school on Academy to Cherokee to Morgan to College to Seminary, and onto the campus to the John Vaughn Library called simply, Library. Sometimes, at College and Seminary, I cut across the lawn and cross the bridge over the Town Branch Creek onto campus under the arch: 1888 Cherokee Female Seminary (Northeastern originally was a seminary where Cherokee girls went to learn Christianity and housework – with an occasional "outing" to work in someone's house), then underneath: Northeastern State University. Then I pass the clock on Seminary Hall (not working) with its numbers in Cherokee. It takes maybe fifteen minutes. It is downhill in the morning; in the afternoon when I'm tired, it's uphill to our house.

I have to rake when it stops raining. The leaves are spirits. When I come back from the library, I'll find another busload from the universe in my yard.

A chalk wolf on the sidewalk.

A mouthful of mothers in the houses I pass.

The library seems like a fort. The rounded boards of my fingers are the stockade wall. The lookout point. I hear the voices in the stacks. The old ones kept there. Closed in the walls of the books. The campground of the ones gone. I hear in truth, but what do I know about it?

My family had a small shelf of books. My father liked books. But there were never many of them.

I remember my mother sick on the couch. Then in bed. The door closed. Then taken somewhere. After a while she came back.

CAPTIVES

That's what the voices are. Captives. Wondering what the imprisonment is about. Maybe the words are the way the voice looks if you could see it. A cloud of insects, their wings opened out, their legs pulled up, they fly into the ears that could hear them. Sometimes I want to swat.

Sometimes I hear the voices of my grandparents. Sometimes I feel the old voices move the way I hear old stories were told without speaking. Even before writing, there were times a story could move without sound. A story was full of variable pieces carried here and there, showing up at different times in different ways, a piece of the story fitting here, a piece there, like furniture moved from room to room, or the same piece changing function according to where it was placed. Always waiting to hear the other factors that were involved that would change the definition. A loose net of words could change in the telling and connect or be swept under to reemerge later, and both the hearer and teller would be changed. All because of the way the story flew and clacked against the side of happenings as though a tree stump in the middle of a river. Somehow I would be thinking about a boat passing the trees along a river, and it would call a story back.

But now there is writing. A book is a disturbance in the pond of my hand. Each page, a wave turning whitecaps on the shore.

In the library, I know a book. I know how it moves. I can hear the waves lapping the shore. Because of the silence of the written word. Books don't talk, though I hear them anyway. The books make a silence in which other things can move.

Look at students reading. It's the old flatboats and steamers on which the voices crossed from the old territory. Reading is the *Smelter* afloat again. A passage the students don't always want to be on.

I even hear the books at night. When I turn out the lights. In my dreams, I see black lines of writing circling the roller rink. Blackgreen as the dark of my sleep. The voices stay with me during the day. I hear them when I'm near the chicken coop of rare books.

But for now, I reshelve the books, help students and researchers find books they need.

KNIFE FIGHT

Robert is wild again when he gets back from another trip. Raymond says something I can't hear. Wayne laughs. Robert has a pocketknife jabbing at his brothers. *What is?* Mary, our mother, says. *The death of me?* I hear the phlung of our father's body between them. Somehow the knife is free. Ether grabs it on the ground. Runs to the car before they see. *Ether,* I cry to him. He runs back, helps my father hold Robert down. I help my mother into the house through the rooms where we once played. Robert jerks away in his truck. I drive back with Ether to our house, crying.

THE DREAM (2)

Am I dreaming?

This my voice (Ada) (somewhere).

Wayne. Whayne. Wain. Where is he? Brother of three. Robert. Raymond. They call Ada. Here we give ride. Push down hill. My ragged doll bump in wagon. Hold on. Ha! They pick up from overturned.

Mother wrap knee, but three. Robt. Raymd. Whain. They hold doll from me. Say, cry. Cry.

Whack them, God! Get brothers of thee.

Bumpy they call. Come get. I always believe.

God, what?

The brothers. They way over (in other lane). Oncoming.

Now this a new paragraph.

I couldn't *stood* much. *The boat rocking. The river roosting. That crowing down the road. It (   ) across the valley.*

This my voice (Ada) Girls!

Going somewhere.

Noel. Nolie. They chair by door. One sleep again. Sitting up. Ether turn page. Nolie jump.

It fever. Sores on the face. Shores of them.

They sit ready to go. Isn't time. Their bags at door. Ether reads the paper.

The only sound his turning page. Girls on sofa. Their knees cross, their chins rest in hands. Noel's hand twitch when Ether turn page. The noise puller back from sleep.

Sleep this wildlife. This brothers' refuge. Given them.

Robert plung knife in brother. Can't wait. I see. Not which. I think this always happen. But not. I wink. They foot on road. Can't go around. Go I wait. They vapor in the valley. It is *I* plug knife in them.

Fever sickness. Lay them on the shore. Upriver. The brothers. The trinity of them.

Cry, they say. Cry for thy dinner, Supper Bell.

THE LOST BOYFRIEND

Noel has had a boyfriend, Wes Stand, since grade school.

NOLIE: "Where's my boyfriend?"

ADA: "*In first grade, the little people moved him away.*"

ETHER: "I'll be your boyfriend."

NOLIE: "It's not the same."

STU: "I'll be – "

NOLIE: "You and Noel had boyfriends since grade school."

ADA: "Someone will find you."

Nolie roller-skates with boys at the rink, but none of them stick. She doesn't mind skating by herself, or with other girls, but she worries about her name.

NOLIE: "You knew your name would be Ronner. Noel knows her name will be Stand. What will my name be?"

I worry that Nolie will throw herself at anyone.

Why doesn't Wes have a younger brother?

Wes *art decks* his car with more fishing lures. He keeps the old propeller from an outboard motor.

ETHER: "If Noel traveled in a spaceship twenty years, how old would she be when she returned?"

The girls: "Dad."

It's my voice in relationship to other voices. Ether, my husband. Noel and Nolie, my daughters. My parents. My brothers. Their wives and children.

I have my family, my church, my work at the Northeastern Oklahoma State University library while Ether teaches physics.

Sometimes I think Ether is lost in the stars.

But slow as shivers, he torches my neck.

THE OUTING

I sit at the table in the small kitchen in my parents' house. My mother is sick again. I am reading – turning pages more than reading. Anything to have in my hands. I can hear my sisters-in-law in the next room. Wayne's wife is talking.

CORA: "I know I should stay married."

I see the words in the book to look at, to think about. The lines come in rows like waves on a shore.

I remember writing patterns with my last name. *No note. No not. Not no. Knower. No knower. No note-er.*

Noel and Nolie are watching the children in the yard:

Robert's daughter and son, Riley and George.

Wayne's son, Stu, and the girls, Clare and Grace.

Raymond's sons, Noah, Tubal, and Caleb.

I keep count to make sure they're all still there.

The leaves are falling like small hands in my parents' yard. With red stems like the string Rahab tied at her window in Jericho's wall.

Noel and Nolie come in from the yard.

ADA: (I sit in the chair the door bumps against. I scrape the chair on the floor moving over.) "Who's watching Stu?"

NOLIE: "Uncle Robert, Wayne, and Raymond."

ADA: "When did they get here?"

NOLIE: "They drove up in Uncle Raymond's van."

The maple leaves bludgeon the yard. Another scrape of the chair.

WAYNE: "I didn't see you there."

ADA: "We grew up in this house without bumping."

WAYNE: "We were smaller then."

ADA: "Noisier, maybe, and we didn't stay long in chairs."

I hope Cora hears Wayne's voice, but Wayne stands by the table listening. Why don't my sisters-in-law know he's here?

I look for Noel or Nolie to warn them, but they are in the other room listening to the women.

RABAH: "If you leave he'll marry someone else. You'll be on your own with Stu and the girls. You'll lose either way."

CORA: "Maybe I already am."

WAYNE: (going into the room) "You got nothing else to talk about?"

The sisters-in-law are startled to see him.

I hear the younger children in the yard in the silence of the house.

I hear Robert and Raymond arguing in the yard. Ether trying to calm them. Noel and Nolie looking at me, now standing in the door. Wayne staring at his wife.

My father comes from the bedroom. My mother is feeling better. He sees Cora and the two sisters-in-law with her. He looks at Wayne.

Ada's father: "I hear your brothers in the yard."

I listen to the sisters-in-law talk after Wayne follows his father to the yard. Why do they get the Nonoter family name while I, a Nonoter, am a Ronner?

THE FORT

After lunch with Ether at the Iguana Café, the head librarian is waiting. There's a meeting about a possible reorganization of books in the library.

I hear the voices again: "We rowed on water. Walked on water. Became the water. Our arms were oars. We still row in boats."

Our stories are made black in the books, written in rows with ink on white pages.

I remember cars in a row as the head librarian talks. The ferry gathering them, taking them away to the other side of the lake, before there was a bridge. When they couldn't cross the water without a ferry. Wes's grandfather worked for the ferry. Wes remembers the water churning white as soap.

I remember other places to escape library meetings: spirits gathering on the hills. Their ball games are lights hit back and forth. They valley out the loose dirt and make a trench where they sit after dark. Those who pass on the road don't see them, though the headlights light their faces like the distant moon.

When Ether went to study physics, I sat in my room. I had to find what I was supposed to do alone. I read. I made a road through the field. I listened. I lived in the books where the rain comes from so high up sometimes it is frozen in winter.

Maybe the spirits I ran into were always cold because they'd traveled so far.

The conjurers are heavy in Cherokee history, but Christianity buffers them. Raymond's wife, Shuba, has conjuring in her family. She's from the Paint Clan – the sorcerers and medicine men. Maybe she keeps Raymond in line with her spells.

When my mother coughs and cannot stop, Shuba works her spell. I hear her out in the yard, walking around the border, saying something.

An old disease brought from Europe. Or was it before that? After work, I walk the house with prayers. The children are choosing their camp which side: conjuring or Christianity.

ADA: "It is not possible, Shuba, to blend them."

THE SKY BLOWING WITH STARS

I believe in truth, which would become a possible truth, which would become the possibilities of truth, which would become the truth of possibilities. Anything to shift the truth from what it is. The history of loss and silence about the loss. I want to open it to shiftings, driftings. I want to fragment the solid block of it.

The language was once circular, existing on land. Embedded in land, in place. Written words strung it out. (Your eyes go back and forth while reading, but the written words pull out into straight narrative.) The way the earth circles for night and day, bowing for seasons, while traveling in a straight path around the sun, which actually itself is curved.

It was not the horse or gun or even Christianity that the new culture brought, but the alphabet.

I look at the night sky. I see the little white letters of its alphabet.

RAKING

Landscape is one of us. Sometimes I think of my family as I rake. Scattering like leaves. The eight nieces and nephews. My two daughters, Noel and Nolie. Wes Stand. They would keep scattering if I didn't rake them back together. Robert's daughter, Riley, his oldest, is already behind him in pursuit.

Maybe the landscape also is an idea. A story. If I look at it that way, I get through the piles of leaves in my yard. They run one way then another, then suddenly change direction. Their continuity is in their always being there, edges curled up like Raymond's handwriting.

Ideas last a while, then pass; books once in demand sit on the shelf; others come, and truth seems to be anyone's. But the library has voices saying our voices are a part of the truth of the land, not truth-for-a-while, but truth that is (something that can't be looked at head-on, like God said to Moses he couldn't).

Sometimes I think I know nothing. I have to remember what I know. The harder I look at truth, the more illusive it is. The more I try to hear the voices in the library, the harder they are to understand.

ETHER: "The universe is full of things we can't see."

I try to change my perspective, but can't. Maybe like Cora not being able to find the frame of mind to remain married to Wayne.

ETHER: "If we could see X rays and gamma rays, they would upset our DNA. The radiation shield that prevents us from seeing keeps us alive."

There is more of it here (landscape): green hills, trees, foliage.

On the Northeastern campus: oak, elm, red mulberry, dogwood.

In winter, there still is land under the infrequent snow.

We began in nature but dumped it for the choice to know the other (the *outside* it); had to regarden what was ours (landscape) turned against us. Landscape (landspace) is a reminder of Adam's fall; the weeds (where were they before?); the animals (predators also) (listen to their growls). The present alienation; tree against tree floating through thought. A turbulence. Disruption upon disruption. We hoe with the decision to decide for ourselves to do what we (thought).

GRACE

I watch the squirrels and birds at the feeder in Wayne and Cora's yard. I can see down into the yard in winter, when the leaves are gone. The small gray birds with white underbellies are juncos. The few times there's snow on the roof of the garage, it is pocked with squirrel tracks. For some reason, I feel a chill.

CORA: "Rabah's right. If I leave Wayne, he'll marry someone else. It's hard on children to be shuffled between families. I see it in my sister's children."

Cora sits in the window seat. The stark light shadows her face. While I listen to her I think, Why haven't I ever felt this?

CORA: "I don't have the heart to stay married. How do you do it, Ada?"

ADA: "I don't know. I just want to be with Ether."

I want to believe my brothers' families will be stable in their own way. I want to believe there is not a single truth but an opening of possibilities. No, I think there is a single truth, but there are smaller truths circling around it.

We come downstairs into the living room. Cora stands at the window.

Grace is Wayne and Cora's younger daughter, their middle child. She is walking down the road with Nolie when some boys run into her with their bicycle.

We hear Nolie scream and run to the door.

NOLIE: "They killed Grace! She's by the road!"

Cora is wild. We run down the road. Cora is speaking a language I haven't heard. It must be a form of Cherokee. We reach Grace and fall at her body.

ADA: "She's breathing."

I tell Nolie to call an ambulance, but a woman yells from her house that she has called. I hold Nolie trembling in my arms. One of the boys has stayed.

THE BOY: (frantic) "We didn't see her."

NOLIE: (yelling in her scared rage) "You did it on purpose!"

I see Nolie's leg is scraped.

NOLIE: "You came hard as you could to scare us."

THE BOY: "No we didn't!"

ADA: "You can't say that, Nolie."

NOLIE: "We heard them laughing. They killed Grace."

ADA: "Grace isn't dead. Get hold of yourself."

The boy rides off on his bike.

NOLIE: (screaming) "Grace killer!"

I slap Nolie to bring her to her senses.

ADA: "You're hysterical, Nolie; calm down."

CORA: "It's Wayne's girlfriend who's done this. She put a spell on me to get Wayne."

Wayne has a girlfriend?

I thought maybe it was Raymond who had the girlfriend.

Maybe Robert who covered the road.

Clare is at school for a scout meeting. Stu is with Noel and Wes. Wayne. Who knows where he is?

We hear the siren coming. Grace's eyes are rolled back in her head. But she's breathing. She's breathing. I put my arm around Cora, who is murmuring. I pat Grace's head and tell her she is all right.

Nolie is still sobbing.

We follow the ambulance to the hospital.

Nolie and I wait while the doctors work with Grace.

CORA: (coming to the waiting room) "She has a broken leg. Maybe internal injuries."

She tries to call Wayne.

THE POLICEMAN: "Who were the boys?"

NOLIE: "I don't know."

Cora slams the phone against the wall in the corridor of the hospital. Wayne is nowhere to be found. But Wes and Noel arrive with Stu. Ether is there also. He comforts Nolie.

Stu begins to understand his sister is hurt and cries.

CORA: "Clare is still at school."

ADA: "We'll get her."

Cora returns to Grace somewhere behind the curtains.

I call Dad, but tell him not to upset Mother.

Noel and Wes take Stu to get Clare from her scout meeting at school, Stu protesting, though he always wants to ride in Wes's car with its fishing lures and outboard motor, his small voice trailing behind him like a wake.

Grace is in surgery when Wayne arrives. Cora comes at him with fury. Ether and I hold her back.

ETHER: "Be calm, Cora. It doesn't help."

She screams at him. Betrayed as a wife and mother, her fury goes beyond the moment.

ADA: "She should be angry."

WAYNE: "I work construction – you know I don't always know where I'll be."

CORA: "Who were you with?"

WAYNE: "Raymond."

CORA: "Well, that's the problem."

THE DREAM (3)

I dream again in the night: a dollhouse library; the books small as fingernails, yet I give Grace two books for crutches.

I remember playing library as a child. But those books I handed out were leaves. They would not stand on a shelf like books, but I stacked them flat on a stand my father made. Was not Sequoyah's syllabary called *Talking Leaves?*

I sat by the road by my parents' house. My brothers, Robert, Wayne, and Raymond, would not take out books. The few cars that came along the road passed without stopping. Only my father took out the *books,* and finally only the imaginary ones, the ancient ones, the squirrels.

Why would I dream of a library? Because I'm a librarian. Is there something else? Yes, I am dreaming words for Grace.

THE TRUTHETTES (1)

The women's Bible study group comes to my house after roller skating. The seven women arrive; three of them, Rabah, Cora (though she will be late), and Shuba, are my sisters-in-law. The other four are friends from church who also roller-skate on Saturday afternoons at Tahlequah Oklahoma's Roller Rink, the Dust Bowl.

My girls, Noel and Nolie, take care of the children upstairs. Ether, my husband, reads and listens for their call if they need his help.

Sometimes my mother comes, but she coughs and everyone's focus is on her.

Rabah and Cora come willingly with the other women to our rollable Bible study on wheels (that is, we meet in one another's houses). Shuba (shoe bug) is reluctant because she deals in conjuring, which she thinks we don't know. But my two girls sit with Shuba's three boys, and they tell me of the medicine bundles they find.

But Shuba knows Christianity has magic too. She has seen the spell of the *born again*. Besides, she is in trouble. Raymond, her husband, is a bundle of anger inside his head. The other brothers, Robert and Wayne, display theirs openly. We also have Grace to worry about.

Sometimes conjuring is nothing more than recognizing the shape of clouds or the choppy waves on a shore when no boat passes, or the way a bird chirps or a squirrel sits on a branch. Sometimes an animal leaves something in the yard.

I begin reading to the Bible study group: "In the night I saw a man riding on a red horse and he stood among the myrtle trees that were in the bottom; and behind him there were red horses, sorrel and white. And I said, what are these? And the man that stood among the myrtle trees answered, The Lord has sent us to walk throughout the earth" (Zechariah 1:8–10).

The chill rises in us. We know these things to be true in Indian country: spirit horses and riders. Could our visions be from God?

ADA: (as Cora arrives from the hospital) "The Lord of hosts has hosts of visions, it seems to me."

The women ask about Grace; then we get back to Zechariah.

Zechariah has other visions. I read about the women with wings like storks; the four chariots:

ADA: "In the first chariot were red horses; and in the second chariot black horses; and in the third chariot white horses; and in the fourth chariot yellow horses. What are these? I ask. An angel answered, They are the four spirits of heaven which go from standing before the Lord of all the earth. The black horses go into the north country; and the white go after them; and the grisled go toward the south country – " (Zechariah 6:1–6).

SHUBA: "Those are visions."

RABAH: "Yes – the four directions."

CORA: "What does it mean?"

SHUBA: "It means whatever it means."

CORA: (reading under her breath) "These that go toward the north country have quieted my spirit in the north country" (Zechariah 6:8).

ADA: "The Cherokees are in a northern county of Oklahoma."

Cora is crying. She must be in a vision. We pray for Grace. There is peace in our study group as we pray. We've studied martyrs. We've prayed for my mother. We've prayed against television. (Shuba can't get her boys away from the television and video games.) We pray for Riley. Rabah senses she is in *flight*. We see a holy light. Beings with great wings holding bowls of something. What is it? Our prayers. We see into heaven. Black horses with beaded manes coming from their stalls. The corrals enclosed with rails of light.

CORA: "It's like watching television." (Cora is crying.) "I see Grace walking again."

ADA: "The visions of Zechariah were like television images that passed before him."

RABAH: "Holy *tele*-vision."

We pray and cry.

ADA: "Even television comes from you. But it is corrupted on earth. Turned into evil. Absorbing people. Sedating them. Lord unload your understanding upon us. Let us see from your viewpoint. Let us see from your holy television."

SHUBA: (she is speaking in the old language) "da:sgino:hiseli."

ADA: "I see leaves flying – pages of the library I used to have (transparent as fingernails). I see the road. Voices of the pages scrambling. The ancient ones stop to read the leaves they take out of my library, looking at one another, nodding, yes, it's yes."

NOW IF I GET THE STORY STRAIGHT

Wayne is furious with the boys who hit Grace, his daughter, with their bicycle.

NOLIE: "It was only one of them who hit her."

Wayne makes her say who she thought it was. He goes to the boy's parents' house. Knocks on the door (this is what I hear later when we're at Mary Nonoter's (my mother's) house).

MARY: "In the old days we was in church all the time. We hung around it whenever we could. We'd get out of school and go to the church. We didn't have revenge in our minds."

SHUBA: "The boy's mother yells at Wayne to go away."

MARY: "When we was married we'd go to church with our babies and quilt. We'd just talk and be there. Nothing like this happened when we was at church."

CORA: "Wayne wants the boy's parents to pay Grace's hospital bills. The boy's parents won't pay the mounting bills. Wayne threatens them. They get a restraining order on Wayne. He files a lawsuit against them."

RABAH: "How are you going to pay for that?"

CORA: "We thought you and Robert could help. He's on the road all the time making money with his rig."

RABAH: "If he is, I don't know about it."
CORA: "You're working too."

Shuba copies a spell from the old records in Manuscripts and Rare Books when I'm not there. She translates it from the old Cherokee and gives it to Wayne to use on the boy's family.

Wayne attacks the house of the boy who hit Grace with his bicycle. He shoots bullets at it. Bullets mixed with a certain root that only Shuba knows (*it has it in its mouth* spell (a certain flower with *an insect in its mouth*)).

The man calls the police. Wayne is in jail overnight.

ADA: "You can't discharge a firearm in the city."

The next morning, the man gets in his truck, drives to the courthouse on his way to work, and files charges against Wayne.

Shuba copies and translates another spell *(to destroy an enemy)* (something like):

bring me   your soul
owl   black   night
night   your name
your heart   it hurts
bring me   your soul
owl   brown, it   night
night   your name
your heart   it hurts

(Bring me your soul. I am a black owl of the night.
Your name is Night. It [the owl] hurts your heart.
Bring me your soul. I am a brown owl of the night.
Your name is Night. It [the owl] hurts your heart.)

When Wayne is out of jail, he returns to the man's house and recites the spell. Over and over. The man comes out of his house. They hit head-on with the force of cars moving fast on the road. Those two going at one another. The crash heard for miles. The impact.

(Those were the spells they used on one another.)

Now Wayne is in jail for several nights. Robert and Raymond and even Ether are with him. They visit as long as the sheriff lets them.

THE BIBLE

I sit in church with Ether. My parents are beside us. Sometimes we round up the nieces and nephews. Cora is with us too. The church is a small, white frame building. There is a row of chairs behind the pulpit for the choir. There are altar benches in front of the pulpit for prayer. Then there are the rows of pews for the congregation. Several sets of windows line the walls. The door is in back. On the two sides of the door are rooms for babies and toddlers. The church has a rectangular shape. It was built half a century ago and has not changed. In the basement is a meeting hall and several Sunday school class rooms. The church has a simple, lasting order, like the Bible that it preaches. But the Bible has stories that lead to other stories and is not always simple. It is a *heat* of stories. Warming up. Such as: all that matters is your attitude to Christ.

Sometimes the stories get broken off from the whole. It's windy when you read the Bible. It's all those voices broken off from the Word, trying to get back to the Word. Sometimes the sermons are like walking through a cloud of whirling insects. Sometimes the sermons blow across the past, loosening it, blowing us back.

Even people are made from stories; they are spoken language made written, made visible. (Our stories say that there was language before there were people.)

What is history but a changing river? (A history seen by its effect on other things.)

There is a road up the hill. I take it because everything is uphill.

AMERICA

They called it the New World, but it was the Old World they came to without knowing.

America has multiple histories, multiple heritages. There's a lot about a lot it doesn't know.

The Indian languages are the history of the continent, if language shapes. Which it does. But we hear the new language (English) at Wayne's hearing, letting him go on probation. (The father of the boy who hit Grace on his bicycle shouting that he'd kill Wayne the next time he saw him in his yard. Ether and Robert guiding Wayne through the crowd before he jumps at the boy's father.)

The trail of Indian civilizations. Older than the Europeans who came. It is under their (the white) houses and highways.

The Peacemaker and the Confederation.

The trade routes.

The wars.

The Great Spirit.

The Christian prayers.

They brought the Western chinking-upward-into-the-pinwheel-universe.

They brought linearity and chronology and getting somewhere and journaling it.

Which probably isn't the point.

But these are the voices:

In the beginning there was a voice. It spoke a language that bore the marks of ruin. Words began bursting into flame. The written words are the ashes of that old flame.

It's the reason there is a moon; it's for the tides so we know how something heavy as the ocean can be moved.

We were a people here for a while, then others came. There were old stories they would come, but not why. There was something we had to know. The Great Spirit seemed (could be saying) (not a throat singer among them). The others named the animals; they named the land (though some of the place names (Tahlequah and Oklahoma) with our own words); they named us, knowing story is the first act.

Why would a people come from far away, saying, *move over?* Their maker brought them here. We know God had them leave their land (why couldn't they stay?) (was thought about as we talked).

Sometimes the old voices get through the *inbetween* our lives trap.

I hear the voices say move over, disembark from keelboats; rebuild bridges, gristmills, sawmills, blacksmith shops, wagon shops, cotton gins, cornfields, orphanages, schools.

I say.
We're inside.
It's inside them.
I think.
That's how it is.

He's got something long.
Friends.
Wool.
Pies.

THE TRUTHETTES (2)

The women gather at my house on Saturday afternoon. They are barbed with troubles. Each in her own way. Unruly children. Distant husbands. Discrimination in their work. Dissatisfaction of one kind or another in their own lives. Some arriving late. Others leaving early to pick up children and/or get various errands done before supper.

I begin the Bible study with something that grabs their attention. I say, roller skating is in the Bible, and I have the women in my open hands. Actually, it's the word *rolling* that's in the Bible.

In the house of Aphrah roll yourself in the dust – Micah 1:10.

Roll the stone from the well's mouth – Genesis 29:8. (Roll the stone from the tomb.)

Then Darius, the king, made a search in the house of the rolls (archives) and there was found in Achmetha, in the province of Medes, a roll, and in it was written (build a temple) – Ezra 6:1–2.

Take a roll and write on it – Isaiah 8:1 (actually it sounds like a library in the Bible).

Then I turned, and lifted my eyes, and behold, a flying roll – Zechariah 5:1

We are in trouble here.

Robert and Wayne and Raymond.

We pray and for the nieces and nephews: Noah, Tubal, and Caleb, Riley and George, Stu, Grace (who has had another surgery on her leg) and Clare, Noel and Nolie.

We pray for my parents.

We pray for the other women's families.

I pray again for Robert. Sometimes I'm afraid he'll just disappear.

We roll into a landscape that is the written word of God. We groan. Cry.

Raymond's wife, Shuba, is probably conjuring while we pray, which is frequent in the Tahlequah Cherokee territory in northeastern Oklahoma.

Though we are Christians now. Except Shuba.

ADA: "But Zechariah doesn't stop with the flying roll. And he said to me, What do you see? And I said, a flying roll. And he said, this is the curse that goes over the face of the earth; for everyone that steals shall be cut off and everyone that swears" (Zechariah 5:3).

SHUBA: "That God of yours is tough."

ADA: "I will enter the house of the thief and the house of him who swears falsely by my name; and it (the curse) shall consume it [the house] with the timber and the stones.

"It isn't you that God is against, but his missiles are sent toward the theft and the lie, and when you do them you call those ground-to-air-missiles that lock into their target."

Shuba leaves the house, angry.

Ada thinks, Well, that might not be the way to get her into league with us. But she has to know what her conjuring will do.

Afterward, Cora serves dessert. Devil's food chocolate. Those small square pieces of cake with icing. How can it be the food of devils? Because it's delicious. Too delicious. Those Satan cakes covered with white icing to hide the darkness beneath. Those white-washed sepulchers. Those tombs.

TO KILL

Wayne keeps making spells against the parents of the boy who hit Grace.

I know it is Shuba working with Wayne. Why can't Raymond, her husband, stop her?

ADA: "No, Wayne. We're in a new place now. Leave those old chants alone. They are still powerful. Like radioactivity that does not go away. If you use those spells, the old world will haunt you. You will be building and slip. You will see conjurers. Animals. Spirits. Hold onto the Word, Wayne. The alphabet is a spaceship with wheels and mud flaps and feathers tied to the rearview mirror. Wayne, hold onto church. It will get you through. There will be an opening. You'll be able to pay your bills."

ETHER: "It will be prison, Wayne, not jail. If you don't leave them alone something will happen."

ADA: "Those spells will create evil for a person. Anything you decide to happen will happen."

THE TRUTHETTES (3)

ADA: "You can't come to the Bible study, Shuba. You can't mix spells and Christianity."

SHUBA: "I'm not – "

ADA: "This is my house, Shuba; you can't come in."

When Shuba storms from the house, we study the martyrs. How they read books with pages that turned to flames. How the lions roared at them, which sounded like mewing in their ears. How Polycarp (who Wes thinks sounds like he should be a fish) dreamed of his pillow on fire and knew he would be burned at the stake. We read how, when they staked him to the wood and burned him, the flames bellied out like a ship's sail in the wind. He was not scorched, but baked like bread.

BED

I sleep by Ether in a bed square as a book. In the night the pages turn. I dream of the old courthouse fire in Sallisaw, where my mother's people lived, burning many of the Cherokee records. I see the words in lines, in rows like corn in a field, except the cornstalks are blackened by fire. In another part of the dream, some of the words have claws, stand-up ears and tails. In another part, the words have a lunch of Spam.

The taillights are campfires.

The spirits turn the lights on and the batteries run down.

The written word, like the spoken, can disappear. But instead of ashes, the remains of written words are rows of barbed wire against the sky.

JOURNAL OF OCCURRENCES

The next day, Manuscripts and Rare Books is busy with students. Late in the afternoon, when I have a break, I look through old Cherokee papers again.

ON THE SECOND ROUTE OF EMIGRATION OF A PARTY OF CHEROKEES FROM ROSS' LANDING E. TENNESSEE TO FORT COFFEE, ARKANSAS

6-6-1838

The Boats having been lashed side by side, 3 on each side of the steam boat, all were got under way about noon and proceeded about 4 or 5 miles an hour. Until we arrived near the Suck when it was necessary to separate them in passing though the mountains. The Suck and Boiling Pot, the Skillet and The Frying Pan are names given to the different rapids formed in the Tennessee River as it passes through the Cumberland Mountains. The river here follows a circuitous course, a distance of 30 miles by water being equal to 8 by land.

The Suck is the first and most dangerous of the rapids. The river here becomes narrow and swift and the banks of either side are rocky and steep, it being the point at which the stream passes thro a gorge in the mountains. The S. boat with one flat on each side passed thro with most of the people on board, but after getting thro the most rapid water, it was found impossible to keep her in the channel, & in consequence was thrown upon the north bank with some violence but none of the people were injured though one of the flats was a good deal mashed.

The other 4 Boats came through two by two and the party was encamped before dark as it was late in the day.

The present party is accompanied by a guard of 23 men in order to prevent any dissertions that might be attempted before leaving the limits of Cherokee Country.

7th June, 1838

The S. Boat and Flat Boats were got under weigh this morning and come thro the remainder of the rapids smartly. The first started at 8 o clock, and all were got thro by noon.

8th June, 1838

Last night being clear and the moon nearly at the full, the Boats continued to run until near daylight when they were obliged to stop and separate owing to the Fog which suddenly arising up. We passed Gunter's Landing about 9 o'clock and then continued to run (stopping once to wood) until dark, when the Boats were landed for the night 6 miles above Decature, and such of the people as choose have gone ashore to sleep and cook. The health has been remarkably fine since starting and the people generally healthy though there are several cases of sickness amongst the children.

June 12, 1838

The movement of a party of Cherokee Indian *comminced* this day from the camp of Four miles distant from the town of Chattanooga, East Tenn. The day was consumed separating the Indians so as to obtain as far as practicable whole families.

June 13, 1838

The party in six flat boats drifted down the Tennessee River to Brown's Ferry, more Indians were this day brought in from camp to increase the detachment (if possible) to one thousand. The Indians express a great aversion to the water route, and want neither to take anything or give up their names.

June 18, 1838

Thomas Jones an assistant conductor was this day attacked with the measles. He was immediately removed from the boat precaution taken to prevent the disease spreading among the indians.

June 21, 1838

Started the detachment at 8 A.M. one very old woman died at Decatur and one man of the 2nd party was killed at the ——— one mile from Tuscumbia. He had been drinking, lost his hat and jumped off the car to obtain it. He was crushed to pieces between Ross Landing and Decatur. 25 Indians left the party. Remained stationary on the Tennessee just below Tuscumbia, waiting the arrival of boats to carry off the party. The detachment became sickly in the opinion of the doctors of the ——— the ——— was in consequence stopped. Two deaths (children).

July 1, 1838

Started at 5 A.M. detained by the fog from ½ past 5 to ½ past 6 A.M. wooded from 1 to 2 P.M. and sheared Paduka Kentucky at ¼ past 8 P.M. for the purpose of obtaining supplies. One death (a child).

July 2nd, 1838

Started from Paducah at 2 A.M. wooded from ½ past 8 to ½ past 9 A.M. detained by a squall of winds from 1 to 2 P.M. and obliged to encamp on the bank of the Mississippi River at ½ past 7 P.M. the river having ——— to a gale and threatening storm.

July 3rd, 1838

The Boats ran all night.

July 4th, 1838

Stopped at Montgomery's Point a few minutes for a pilot, entered White River at 10 min past 8 A.M. the Arkansas River (by the cut off) at ½ past 9 A.M. and encamped on the bank of the Arkansas at 7 P.M. two deaths (children).

July 6, 1838

Started at 4 A.M. and landed the detachment one mile above the city of Little Rock on the opposite bank of the Arkansas River at 3 P.M. the boat was ———ed twenty feet from the shore. A plank thrown out, and the indians made a pass over it singly. They were thus accurately counted and found to number 722 making an allowance of two deaths that occured on the passage.

July 7, 8, 9, 10 & 11, 1838

Remained stationery on the river bank awaiting for a light draft boat to carry the detachment up. Much sickness in the party, diseases measles & summer ——— complaint. S. N. Tunneh (?) arrived on the 11th. Made a contract with the owner Mr. S——— to carry the party on the steamboat and two keels to Ft Coffee or Ft Gibson for the consideration of $5.50 per head, and should the river be too low to ascend or ——— to be paid in proportion to distance.

July 14, 15, 16, 17, 18 & 19

Started the party at 5 A.M. engaged in hiring wagons. Found it diffcult to obtain much as I tried. ——— obliged to hire a ——— and start them 20 & 30 miles in the country. Two deaths.

July 20, 1838

Commenced the movement with twenty wagons, owing to the number of children, and the sick, had to leave about 40 in the camp.

July 21, 1838

Provided more wagons and started the balance, much sicknesss & increasing three four & five deaths per day. Diseases measles and flux caused by the use of green peaches & corn.

July 23, 1838

Started at sunrise, encamped at 12 n at Illinois River to give the party time to beat corn & wash. Much sickness & increasing number of deaths daily.

July 27, 1838

Started the party at sunrise & encamped on White ——— at 12 n Between two & three hundred sick & four & five deaths daily.

July 31, 1838

Started the party at daylight & encamped in Jin's [?] creek at 2 P.M.

Aug 1, 1838

Did not move this day, the party requiring rest and more than one half sick. Notwithstanding every effort was used, it was unprofitable expedient [?] their eating quantities of green peaches & consequently the flux raged among them and carried off some days as high as six or seven. Mr. C. Van authorized by Capt Stephen son to secure the party, met us then, & owing to the great scarcity of provisions in the neighborhood of Ft Gibson, ——— that the party be turned over in the Flint Settlement.

Aug 3, 1838

Started the party at daylight and encamped at the foot of Boston Mountain at 12 n. Much sickness still among the Indians and a number dying daily.

Aug 4, 1838

Started the detachment two hours before day, upon the mountain, entered the C. Nation, and encamped on the head of Lee's creek in the Flint settlement at 12 PM.

Aug 5, 1838

Turned over the detachment to Mr. C. Van as directed by Capt. Stephen son and found the party as follows:

602 Indians present

65 Indians left the party and went into the Nation after arriving on the line

70 deaths on the Journey

Total distance 1554

R. H. K. Whetily [?]
Lt. U.S.A.

THE *OBSERVER*

In the evening, I'm reading the *Cherokee Observer.* How Cherokees used to make floats of deerskin and bearskin. Sometimes they'd wrap their gear inside, knot the shanks of the skins, and swim across the rivers.

Cora is at the door before I finish the newspaper article. She has Stu, Grace, and Clare. She wants Noel and Nolie to watch them and leaves before I tell her the girls aren't here.

CLARE: "She's going after dad."

STU: "He's with somebody."

Stu knows something I don't? Why don't I know what's going on?

ADA: "They should have kept Wayne in jail."

Ether is grading papers in his study. The girls are shopping. Wayne's children can help me with supper. When the girls come back, they can help wrap the gifts. It is nearly Christmas.

STU: "What are you eating for supper?"

ADA: "I think some chili. You want some?"

He does.

ADA: "Do you want a cracker while we fix it?"

He does.

I ask the children to toss the salad, butter the bread, and ice the carrot cake. I see Stu licking the icing off his finger.

Grace sets the table, and Clare pours water in the glasses. Stu is still icing his hands.

CLARE: "Here, Stu, you're getting it all over yourself."

She tries to take his butter knife away, and he protests with a loud wail.

Just then the girls come in the backdoor with their packages and Stu runs to them. Noel and Nolie are in the Pendleton coats they got for their birthday. They scream when they see Stu's hands. I pull him away from them and wipe his hands.

ADA: "Ether! We're ready to eat." (I yell.)

Clare and Grace tell us their mother knows where Wayne goes. She is following him.

Ether looks at me.

After supper, the children help Noel and Nolie wrap Christmas gifts while Ether and I clean.

Later, I read about illegal dumping, loan agreements, embezzled funds, and the last of the historical article in the *Observer.*

Christmas is a grim occasion. After Cora finds Wayne, they have an argument in front of his girlfriend's house. The neighbors call police and I read about it also in the *Cherokee Observer.*

Mother is sick and Dad is sullen. Robert and Rabah arrive with Riley and George. Wayne brings the three children. Grace's eyes are red. Raymond and Shuba come with Noah, Tubal, and Caleb. Wes is there also.

OBED: "Where is Cora?" (My dad is growing angry.)

WAYNE: "She's not coming."

OBED: "I never acted this way. I never hurt my family."

WAYNE: "When I want to know what you think, I'll ask."

My father is furious and tears into Wayne. It takes my two brothers and Ether to separate them.

MARY: (crying) "Stop! Stop."

Wes is holding Noel and Nolie, who are holding Grace, Clare, and Stu.

Rabah, Shuba, and I serve dinner quickly. We eat in silence, except for Raymond's three boys.

I'm afraid Cora will come and cause another scene, but the evening passes without her.

All are quiet as they open their gifts, except Stu and Raymond's three boys.

I listen to a few comments but don't speak.

I watch everyone gather coats and gifts, thanking one another; the guests leave; Robert and Rabah helping Mary and Obed out the door.

Later I call Cora and wish her a new season.

THE TRUTHETTES (4)

We continue with fire in our Bible study through an ice storm late in January.

ADA: "The king sat in the winter house [Jeremiah 36:22], and there was a fire in the hearth burning before him. And when Jehudi read three or four columns (of the word of the Lord that Jeremiah, the prophet, had written on a roll), Jehoiakim, the king, (not liking what he heard) cut it with the knife and cast it into the fire until the roll was consumed.

"And the word of the Lord came to Jeremiah [Jeremiah 36:27–28] after the king had burned the roll and said, take another roll and write the former words that were in the first roll which Jehoiakim, the king of Judah, burned."

SHUBA: (she shows up anyway) "That's what I'd do."

After fire, we move to unclean animals (Leviticus 11) that should not be eaten: the eagle, ossifrage, osprey, vulture, falcon, raven, ostrich, night hawk, sea gull, white owl, cormorant, horned owl, swan, pelican, eagle, stork, heron, hoopoe, bat, and all winged insects (fowls that creep) (creak).

THE OKLAHOMA TWISTERS (WHIRLWINDS)

We skate at the roller rink. Riley and George, Stu and Clare, Noah, Tubal, and Caleb, Noel and Wes, Nolie, even some of Wes's cousins. Grace can't skate; may not be able to skate for a long time because of her leg brace, yet she insists on coming to the Dust Bowl. One by one, we sit with her as she watches us skate, except Riley, who is busy skating with the boys.

What a clan. A photo booth full of us.

I remember Ether at the drugstore where he swept up. Afterward, he was off watching swirls in the sluggy river, holding a string to watch resistance in the water moving forward.

We would watch one another at a dance but not dance. When he went to college, I stayed in the library.

In those days, we'd drive sometimes to the Holy Roller Rink near Grove, Oklahoma, fifty miles north.

ADA: (I say to Nolie) "Think of Ether's relativity. Circumstances can shift and you'll have a boyfriend." (The boy (Nolie's boyfriend) who moved away in first grade could move back.)

NOLIE: "But would he be the same? If my father's theory is correct – if someone travels in space, they'd be the same age on return."

Nolie looks at the first-grade boys at the roller rink.

REVELATION

I hear distant skating in the sound of a pencil on paper in the library as the students write notes for their papers. Sometimes it's as frightening as the sound of a windstorm. It's as if the tornado and destructive voices were drawn into the library by the act of writing. A ceremony turned upside down. It is what church, also, is actually about. War. I hear it in the library. Raymond's wife, Shuba, conjuring. A piece of paper. Someone taking notes. Copying a spell. The paper later found. But it's Raymond's handwriting. It's Raymond's!

ADA: (later) "Raymond – what's the matter with you? You know those spells have power. You remember in the book of Daniel [10:10–21], when he prayed, and the spirit, the angel, who arrived later, said he couldn't get through the air, though he heard Daniel's prayer from the beginning? The prince of the air over Persia [which is where Daniel was at the time] prevented him from passing for two weeks, until Michael, the bigger angel, came and helped him. There're spirits over countries, over places, over words. You know there's a warfare above us. There are two opposite camps. You were with me in Sunday school. You know the two sides fight over us. Remember how we heard the spirits as kids? Out there in the open? On the hill? We knew they were fighting above us. Remember how we could feel the electricity? You are giving yourself to conjurers, to the dark ones,

Raymond. Those spells have magic. They make things happen. Just like the words of prayer. You are plugging your cord into their socket. It's the old war: the dark ones against the light. You are choosing the dark."

I see Raymond turn pale as I talk. I feel my hair stand up. The spirits are above us now. Our words drew them to us. Our words are magnets for their energy. The dark powers don't want me talking to Raymond.

ADA: "You're choosing conjuring over Jesus."

RAYMOND: "Be quiet, Ada."

ADA: "You feel them too – "

LEVIATHAN

In church, I listen to the minister read from Job 41. But I hear *library* instead of *leviathan.*

MINISTER: "Can you catch a library with a hook? Can you pierce its skin with barbed irons, or its head with fish spears?"

Job had been a librarian. In Manuscripts and Rare Books. I knew it. He was in the middle of library reorganization. Overworked. Stressed.

MINISTER: "Who can open the doors of its face? Its teeth are terrible. One book is so near to another, no air can come between them. By its sneezings a light shines. Out of its mouth go burning lamps and sparks of fire. Out of its nostrils goes smoke. Its breath kindles coals. Its pages are joined together; nothing can come between. It is firm as a stone, as hard as a piece of the millstone. It makes the deep to boil like a pot. It makes a path to shine. Upon earth, there is nothing like it."

THERE IS A VOICE I DON'T LISTEN TO

The Nonoters are the Deer Clan, the clothes makers. I remember playing with the girls in the playhouse my father made for them. We cut out paper doll clothes with tabs on their shoulders. The wind blew around them like kites. (The girls would find them in the neighbor's yard.)

NOLIE: "Now the playhouse in the backyard is for the little people."

Except Grace and Clare play there. Sometimes Raymond's boys attack it like a fort. Or a keelboat. They take an oar Wes is trying to put on his art car, and row from the window of the little house.

SHUBA: (when she comes for the boys and sees them rowing) "How do they know about keelboats?"

ADA: "Our words blow us into ourselves. Not away, no, but into the landscape of language we carry in our head. The past is caught in that net somehow (those branches of words). We uncover it as we talk. The magic of the written word is in the Bible we study – it renews us – it enters our lives, Shuba, we become like it."

SHUBA: "Cora is a Christian. What good does it do her?"

THE DISPOSSESSED

I stand in the library from time to time looking through the books. Some of them don't speak, but the words remain in their rows to be picked like corn. I step into their field and harvest the reading.

Our stories are kept now in books. That's why I like the library. Ordered (unlike family). Shelved. Rowed. But even that is subject to change and reordering.

Even in the books that don't speak, I feel the old territory. I feel the trail, not the overland march, but the crossing from the old territory by water. It's the way my ancestors must have come. Even in the night, don't I feel the rowing? Don't I hear them refusing to give their names to the soldiers, to the roll takers? Didn't I hear them refusing to take anything with them? Some know they will die. Don't I feel the movement of the boat over the water? Don't Ether and I row together?

We are the dispossessed; the Cherokees who were here before DeSoto came. I feel the old anger at being moved from our land. Is this, only much more of it, what Robert, Wayne, and Raymond feel? Maybe I have it too. Where is it for me? Covered by the gospel?

CRYING IS MY RIVER (PSALM 42)

ADA: "Where is God?"

I've prayed for years for Robert, Wayne, and Raymond. For their wives, Rabah, Cora, and Shuba. For their children, Riley and George, Grace, Clare, and Stu, Noah, Tubal, and Caleb. Why did Christianity sink into me and not my brothers?

Maybe it's an old voice I hear. A voice praying and praising God on the river trip. When everything looked hopeless. There was smallpox. There was a voice that carried faith.

I know the murmuring I hear in the library is the old Cherokee (like Old English is different from what we hear now). The old language is stronger than what the nieces and nephews learn in school. I can hear the difference. (In the book of Ezra, when the temple was rebuilt, the ones who had not seen the previous temple cheered, but the ones who remembered the old temple wept (Ezra 3:12).)

Maybe the old Cherokee sounds to me like the Bible sounds to Shuba (someone outside its language).

I hear Robert disrespectful to his wife. Raymond and Shuba arguing. Cora crying at the meeting of the Truthettes. Raymond's three boys have pulled down the stacked cordwood stacked again. They run wild through the house. Grace withdraws into herself. I see Riley drive by with boys too old for her. George kills a small squirrel. Nolie holds it in a box on her lap. Why did it have to die? Her voice sticks on the page I am reading. George stunned it with a rock. It was flopping in the yard. He speared it with a stick. George curses Nolie.

GEORGE: "They're mean. They have to die!"

He runs out of the house and down the street when she starts after him. The storm of family is always overhead. Thunderheads. I cry when I think of them. I am angry. I feel helpless. Sorrowful. A thought comes: Why am I crying? It is the way Jesus feels. He cries over us. Sometimes when I am brought to a moment of realization, I cry also, out of the recognition of it. Out of the holy significance of our lives. Nolie returns to the house and slams the door. We are both crying. We go to the backyard and bury the squirrel.

It is the benefit of a disrupted family. You never want to go back. It is a mix of wanting to move on and having to reach back to pull them with you.

I remember a Sunday school teacher with a fat, unloving wife, a low-paying job, yet somehow he held on.

UNTITLED (1)

Noel graduates from high school and Ether wants her to go to the University of Oklahoma, but she wants to stay in Tahlequah with Wes, who is going to Northeastern.

ETHER: "You'll have to live with us. Everyone else wants to leave home."

NOEL: "I do too, but Wes is staying here."

ETHER: "You could go without him. Your mother and I were in separate places for college."

NOEL: "Yes, and weren't you happy about it."

UNTITLED (2)

Wayne and Cora are divorced. The children cry when they stay with me that afternoon.

ADA: "It will be all right."

Grace still limps in her leg brace as she comes to me with a book, the tears drying on her face in faint white streaks.

I feel her small body quiver as I hold her on my lap.

ADA: "Noel and Nolie will take you for ice cream."

GRACE: "Momma." (She sucks air in a quiet sob.)

I read Grace a story about a man and a bear. I read how the man went hunting and shot the bear. But it was a medicine bear who could talk and read the thoughts of men. The bear invited the man to his house, which was actually a cave full of old bears, young bears and cubs, white bears, black bears, brown bears, and a large bear who was the chief. The bears saw the man's bow and arrows and said, let's see if we can manage them, but their long claws caught in the bowstring and the arrows dropped to the ground. In the spring the bear said to the man, other hunters will come and kill me. They will take you back to your settlement, but when they do, look back and you will see something.

When the hunters came, the dogs found the cave and began to bark.

They dragged the bear outside and killed it and skinned the body and covered the blood with leaves. When the man followed the hunters back toward the settlement, the man looked back and saw the bear rise up out of the leaves, shake himself, and go back into the woods.

THE DREAM (4)

A book is a story in a bag dress or one of those sleepers (jumpers) that are a square with openings for feet, hands, head, wings. These are the books: Robert Nonoter, Wayne Nonoter, Raymond Nonoter. But their actions overwrite the pages, change the text, tear out whole pages.

At the skating rink, I tell Robert: "Be careful."

At the skating rink, I tell Robert my dream about tearing out pages.

ADA: "That's what your actions do: lessen your book you will carry into the hereafter."

ROBERT: "I don't like a book already written on."

ADA: "There are blank pages, maybe more than the written. But there are some pages you can't change, can't write on: to do so is to lose part of yourself."

Robert follows as I skate in the roller rink arena, but I am thinking of books:

A book is a (hear)t.

A book is a neighborhood.

A book is a m(arina) of docks for keelboats.

A book is a m(art)yr.

A book is (scratchy as) a wax cylinder recording those ethnographers made.

A book is flames.

Robert and I pass Ether while the nieces and nephews pass us on both sides, their hair blowing like pages of books, their eyes hard as bindings.

Over us, I see (library) books in bag dresses; they open their hardcover wings, glide above the wind currents of the skaters. A book is a hi(story). A book is a ho(ax). A book is (magi)c. A book is silent, yet it tells a story. But a book is not God.

ADA: "Do you remember the bus trip?"

ROBERT: (with George and Riley skating around him) (Riley is now taller than Robert) "The bus trip?"

ADA: "When we were at Grandpa's and the tree limb fell on the car?"

ROBERT: "The tree didn't hurt the car – we took the bus because Dad was going to leave the car for Grandpa."

ADA: "No – "

ROBERT: "Don't you remember the car at Grandpa's?"

ADA: (irritated) "Yes, but that was before the tree fell on it."

ROBERT: "No – after."

ADA: "Riley – you're going to trip us – I don't want to fall."

ROBERT: "I think the little people are moving your thoughts around."

BUFFALO COOKIES

I sit at my parents' house looking through the old photo albums. Mary, my mother, has been sick for years. She does not want to go to the other world because of the turbulence of her sons, but she is not going to be able to stay much longer.

She keeps the old albums in a drawer. I look through them. I take one into her room when she calls.

ADA: "I see the four of us lined up at the Ford. Underneath: Rbt. Wyn. Rymd. A. Do you remember the old Ford?"

MARY: "Yes. Reuban, your grandpa, finally got it. He borrowed a lot from your dad."

ADA: "But didn't a tree limb fall on the car?"

MARY: "Obed never would stand up for himself."

ADA: "I remember a tree limb on the car."

MARY: "Yes – I remember. (She laughs and coughs and cannot stop. Robert has not left yet in his truck for the road he comes into the room we sit her up hold her until where's Dad? In the yard sitting by himself cannot hear *Dad* we call her coughing is a storm. What limb has fallen now? We let her head rest on the bed when the storm lets up her chest heaves again we lift she coughs until she stops we let her down. Robert stays a while then leaves the room.)

I sit by Mary while she sleeps or rests. I look through the album again. Reuban and my grandmother. Obed and Mary. Robert, Wayne, and Raymond standing stiffly or horsing around. Ada in a new dress holding her books ready for school. Photos of a young Ether. The girls as babies.

Later my mother says:

MARY: "The car was Reuban's when the tree got it."

I put my hand on her mouth. I don't want her to talk, to be stirred by whatever happened. I remember a storm when the car was ours. A tree fell on it in Reuban's (Grandpa's) drive. The car was dented. I remember the roof of the car nearly pushed down to the seat. No one but the little people could drive it. That's the way I remember it. That's the way it was.

We take turns doing what we can. Wayne. Raymond. The grandchildren visit. The church elders. Shuba's conjuring. (I see one of her feathers at my mother's bed but don't ask when she was here.)

Even Cora comes with her own storm. Someone is putting a curse on her, she says. Shuba, she suspects, because she won't stay out of Wayne's way and maybe Raymond has asked her to. Cora won't let Wayne live with his girlfriend in peace. Why should she? She questions whenever I see her. Her voice rising at the Iguana Café or on the street or in the market or wherever we speak.

MARY: (another afternoon (she speaks now in whispers)) "The lines in your books go back and forth, Ada. I want to circle."

ADA: "I'm going to read to you anyway." (I read to my mother from Psalms.)

MARY: "I hear them at night."

ADA: (I stop reading) "Who?"

She doesn't answer.

ADA: "Mom?"

MARY: "I hear Grandma and Grandpa. My parents. They're getting ready. They're preparing a feast. Someone is coming."

I don't know what to do. I think of something else. A book has no legs. It doesn't eat or get tired like a horse. Yet it goes anywhere. A book carries a story without speaking. Imagine the transfer of language overland if all it had was a voice.

MARY: "I don't know what it'll be like."

ADA: "You made cookies in the shape of buffalo, Mother. You've never seen them either."

MARY: "You take care of them, Ada."

ADA: "I do. But I expect Robert, Wayne, and Raymond to be responsible for their own families too."

MARY: "I grieve over them."

ADA: "I see books with hands floating from them. The hands are reaching Noel and Nolie, George and Riley, Grace, Clare, and Stu, Noah, Tubal, and Caleb."

The written word must miss the voice. Words have to be quiet in writing. Maybe it is in mourning that words are written straight on the page, stiff with sorrow as an umbrella handle. But stories had to go farther than ears could hear. But the words must have asked, Would a story still be a story without the voice to tell it? With only the eye to see it? A written story is the voice walking where the spoken story could not reach.

Ether is with me now; the family in the other room, no one fighting for once. The brothers come in one by one. Then their families. The younger grandchildren asking what's wrong with Grandma, their mothers hushing them. The older children crying. Even Cora has come. Wayne must have left his girlfriend in the car. Wes comforts Noel. Nolie stands between Ether and me. It is my father who has said nothing.

THE WAKE

We hold the wake for my mother in the meeting hall of the church. She is in the open coffin in the middle of the room. We sit in a circle around her. Some leave her gifts. Some speak. The women cook. From time to time we get up for something to eat.

ROBERT: (at first, he can't speak) "She died in her sleep."

WAYNE: (he is broken up also) "Somehow she let go."

RAYMOND: "She kept the peace."

ADA: "She came to the last page and her book closed."

GRACE: (sobbing) "Grandma."

ADA: "My mother always did what she wanted. In grade school, when I played the triangle in the band, she sold buffalo cookies for our band trips, though the Cherokees did not hunt buffalo. The Cherokees were corn farmers, but that didn't make any difference to my mother, nor the people who bought the cookies." (The people laugh.) (Actually, she reminds me of the mural inside Seminary Hall called *The Buffalo Hunters;* not that the mural belongs there, but other native students (other than Cherokee) attend the university (the Kiowa, who did hunt buffalo, for instance).)

OBED: "She's with her parents and grandparents – her family before her that I didn't know. The mothers are honoring her."

ADA: "Yes, I hear them – they are with her. The ancestors. Those who died on the trail – in the rowing. They came for her. They are talking now."

NOEL: "She was our grandma."

Afterward, I go roller skating. (She would want me to.)

CHURCH CAMP

I hear Noel and Nolie; their full-blood, half-blood, mixed-blood heritage, erased, diluted, blended, rerouted: the library voices of the girls and their cousins and friends. They are an oral narrative, a written narrative. Their voices emerge as they speak, uncurling from the cocoon like a butterfly with its markings of scaffolding and paint splatters.

The voice is the wings in the story's air. In spite of gravity, Ether's favorite force.

NOEL: (as she makes her bed at church camp) "I like the smell of my father's glasses; the parts that go behind his ears."

NOLIE: "I like the smell of Noel's pillow when it's my turn to change the beds."

It's the church campground: the kitchen and eating hall, the cabins, the meeting hall open to the air because of the heat. There is dust. It is high summer though it's still June.

Church camp is the resistance movement to television, drugs, alcohol, and the other problems that pull them off the road.

Noel and Nolie don't question church camp. Grace and Clare only want to do what Noel and Nolie do. Riley doesn't want to do anything we do.

Nolie is preoccupied. She's late to meetings. Her attention wanders. Her enthusiasm is gone. She isn't interested. Something else is going on. She can't sit in one place, while Noel can spend the day reading.

ADA: "Who are you, Nolie? What are you thinking?"

NOLIE: "What do you mean?"

ADA: "You seem distracted. You get up several times, leave, and return. Like wind lifting the dust on the road."

NOLIE: "Not everyone is the same."

ADA: "Do you miss Grandma?"

Nolie nods. "I'm not Noel."

ADA: "I don't want you to be. Wandering is a distraction. Hang on, Nolie, through the hard part. Look at Grace and Clare watching you. Don't you see them looking for someone to follow? Maybe even Riley looks to you."

NOLIE: "Don't count on it."

ADA: "She's here with us, isn't she?"

A STORY WITHIN A STORY

I bring an old book from the library – a copy of an old book, rather, because the actual book cannot leave Manuscripts and Rare Books. We read through the story as a drama, with Noel and another girl present at church camp: *Poor Sarah, or Religion Exemplified in the Life and Death of an Indian Woman.*

NARRATOR: "It was a cold morning, March 1814, when I met Sarah.

She called to ask for a few crusts, saying meekly, she desired nothing but the crumbs – they were enough for her poor old body, just ready to crumble into dust."

The story was written by the Cherokee leader, Elias Boudinot, born in 1802 in Georgia. His parents sent him to a Moravian mission school, where he learned English. Later, he became the editor of the *Cherokee Phoenix,* the first Indian newspaper. He also signed the 1835 Treaty of New Echota, which removed the Cherokees to the west by boat and the overland trail. On arrival in Indian Territory (Oklahoma) he was murdered along with Major Ridge and John Ridge, the other two Cherokee chiefs who had signed the treaty.

ADA: "His story about Poor Sarah is so long, Noel, they won't listen. We have to shorten it."

NOEL: "How can you do that?"

ADA: "We hear a story, retell it in our own way."
NOEL: "I don't want to."
ADA: "I think you should make it your own."
NOEL: "Then it will be your presentation instead of mine."

POOR SARAH (1)

SARAH: "When the night come, husband come home angry beat me so, then I think, O if Sarah had friend, Sarah no friend; I no want to tell nabor I got trouble, that make only worse. So I be quiet, tell nobody, only cry all night and day for one good friend. One Sunday, good nabor come, and say, come Sarah, go meetin. So I called my children, tell 'em stay in house, while I go meeting. When got there, minister tell all about Jesus; how he was born in stable; go suffer all his life, die on cross, bury, rise, and go up into heaven."

While I'm listening to the girls read Poor Sarah, Ether comes to the room.

ETHER: "Cora called the camp. Wayne saw the family of the boy who hit Grace on his bicycle. He made a scene. Later he borrowed Raymond's van and ran over the boy's bicycle. The family filed further charges. Could you come back to Tahlequah?"

ADA: "I'm staying at camp."

THE DREAM (5)

Books form a record around us. . . . They are . . .
the living animals themselves.

In Defense of the Book, William Gass

While I am at church camp (and Wayne is rearranging Tahlequah), Northeastern State University is reorganizing the library; moving genealogy downstairs, reshelving the books. Everything is changing places. Everything but Manuscripts and Rare Books. It will stay in the chicken coop and the other older books will remain in their upstairs corner.

I dream of the books. I hear them in the night. I want to be with them – comfort them. The old books feel the move. But they must know they are not moving. Why do they speak more than they did? There is something else happening. They are mourning. What?

I dream there is another reorganization. Just as the books of written words replaced the stories of spoken words, something would replace the books. That's what it was. Didn't the head librarian say that new orders for film and video were more in number than for books? Didn't students get their information now off the Internet more often than not? The books, the written words, were crying because they realize the possibility that they will be replaced.

The next day, I jerk with a start. I am holding Grace on my lap, though she is too big. That is the message! That's why I hear the voices more often now. Grace looks at me. I tell her I am thinking; she should listen to the girls rehearse *Poor Sarah.*

Just as the written word is a splinter of the voice, maybe the words written on a computer screen are a splinter of the words written in a book. Or maybe it's the book that's the splinter of the words moving on the screen. At least the collection of audio books in the library picks up on the oral tradition.

Nonetheless, the Internet is something not expected. It startles the books in the library, especially the books in Manuscripts and Rare Books. The way I hear birds when a storm is coming. The books know their own storm is near.

> Off the screen they do not exist as words. They do not wait to be reseen, reread; they only wait to be remade, relit. I cannot argue in their margins; I cannot . . . return to find the jam I . . . smeared . . . still spotting the page.
>
> *In Defense of the Book,* William Gass

> the page, the square cover, the sewn edge, the table . . .
> disappearing edges . . .
> the book is coming apart.
>
> *Juan Gris / le livre,* Kazim Ali

A FRAMED NARRATIVE

I watch Noel and her friend read the part of Narrator and Sarah.

Grace sits on my lap again. I think she is at the bottom of her life. There is a heaviness on her like a keelboat.

ADA: "You don't know the next self you will be. Do you understand, Grace? The way you feel is not the end, but something you are passing through."

She hears but doesn't answer.

She is wearing a pair of white gloves the girls were going to use for the narrator. But they are too small. Grace pulls them off because her hands are hot. There are seam lines along her fingers.

ADA: "You see those lines on your fingers? Do you know what will happen to them? They will disappear like your unhappiness."

Grace shakes her head, yes, and I see tears run down her face.

POOR SARAH (2)

NARRATOR: "Sarah was in the habit of bringing bags of sand into the village, and selling them. You might often have seen her hands uplifted, in the attitude of prayer. One day, after having observed her as she came, I asked her how she could bring such heavy loads, old as she was, & feeble."

SARAH: "O, when I get great load, then I go pray God give me strength to carry."

The audience squirms, but the girls get through the beatings, the poverty, the unchanging husband, the disobedience of Sarah's children, her old age and death. They get through the long, sorry tale, sorry except for Sarah's hope of resurrection and reward.

Afterward I make a late call to Cora.

Now Wayne has to pay for a new bicycle for the boy and face another hearing.

ETHER'S TESTIMONY AT CHURCH CAMP

ETHER: (looking at Ada) "I change transparencies on the overhead projector. I hear the low whir of the machine like turning pages of a book, or little waves lapping at the shore, or the bottom of the fishing boat.

"I could think I was on the lake with my tackle box, net, reel, and when I turn the projector off, there's a lonely silence. It is the light waves of the projector that define grace.

"You take multivariable calculus (no longer looking at Ada). The speed of light throughout the universe is constant. Something like time has to slow down to compensate. Matter has wavelike properties. Sometimes definitions are based on probabilities. For instance, neutrinos are small particles that don't have mass. But it was just discovered that they do have mass."

I am looking at the roof of the pavilion where we sit in the heat. Noah, Tubal, and Caleb are turning rowdy behind me. Ether now thinks he is in the lecture hall. But somehow, he comes to himself. Space and time no longer bend for the mass of his testimony.

Afterward, I hear him talking to Nolie.

NOLIE: "It's the two different answers to the same equation that bother me."

ETHER: "Think of a bouncing ball. Its place in space is based on whether it's on its way up or down, or wherever it is in its arc."

I see Tubal watching Ether, his little eyes like neutrinos that have just found their mass.

THE FIGHT

Noel is impatient with Wes. He is busy herding the boys. He is not paying enough attention to her. She sulks. He does not realize it at first. He thinks she is busy with the girls (which she is.) She snaps at him. He does not understand. He withdraws. It is the very thing he should not do. She snaps again. She is asking for his attention.

ADA: "We are born into peace [I tell Noel] by the blood of Christ. Wes loves you. Don't provoke him. Belittling one another becomes a habit. Haven't you seen your aunts and uncles?"

CLOSE

The boys are jumping on their bunk beds. Ether and Wes are trying to get their clothes into their duffel bags, their blankets folded up, their wet towels and swimming trunks dried as we prepare to leave the church camp. Caleb jumps higher than he realizes and cracks his head on the bed above him. There's a gash above his forehead. I hear him scream and I run to their cabin.

Ether is lifting Caleb's eyelids and Caleb, fortunately, wants Ether to leave him alone.

ETHER: "I think he passed out for minute."

Ether and I borrow the minister's car, which doesn't start at first, just like the church bus. We take Caleb into town, about twenty miles away, where there's a clinic. Caleb is still screaming. Blood is running down his face and neck. He wants his brothers. He wants his mother and father. He wants God, he says.

Ether stays with the doctor and Caleb. I am on the phone calling his mother for permission to take stitches. I cannot get her. I remember the permission forms the church campers have to fill out. I call the camp kitchen, the only place with a phone. The cook finds the minister, who finds the paper. He talks to the nurse. The doctor proceeds with the stitches. I stay in the waiting room. I hear Caleb calling Jesus.

People in the waiting room look at me.

ADA: "We're from church camp."

Ether and Caleb come from the emergency room. Caleb's head is wrapped. The front of his head shaved. He is holding a toy car.

The doctor wants him to stay in the clinic overnight, but we are on our way home, Ether explains. We'd have to bring all the kids. We're packed and ready to leave camp.

ETHER: "We'll watch him. No, we won't let him sleep. Yes, we'll take him to the doctor when we get back to Tahlequah."

We return to camp. Caleb's brothers and cousins are lined up to see him. Caleb's eyes are still red from crying. His forehead swollen. His head is starting to bruise. The boys want to see under Caleb's bandage, but Ether says not yet.

Wes, Noel, and Nolie have all the duffel bags and bedrolls lined up at the edge of the parking lot. They load the bus and Ether drives away from church camp. I sit behind him holding Caleb on my lap, bouncing him if he looks like he is sleepy. Noel and Nolie hold Raymond's other two boys. Wes has George. Riley, Grace, and Clare are supposed to watch the rest of the bus. We've had a hard time getting everyone packed up. The cousins keep fighting. Even Stu. Ether says this is the last time we're bringing any of them to church camp, but he says that every year.

ADA: (as the old bus rocks onto the road) "I feel like we are rowing a keelboat, not sure we'll make it." (The bus usually breaks down on the way to camp or from it – sometimes both.) Yes, it's the old tribe on the river.

Somehow the boys quiet down. I talk to Caleb to keep him awake.

ADA: "I dream I'm flying with a star. It has wings that open out like leaves on your mother's table."

I feel the bus glide over the road. Ether has it on a downhill roll. We're making time.

THE REBUILT

When we return from church camp, Cora has moved in with my father. Ether and I drop off Stu, Clare, and Grace at Dad's. Wayne is there too. He has followed us to see where we're taking the children. Wayne has a fit in Dad's front yard. Dad won't let him in the house. If he won't take care of his family, then my father will. Ether and I try to talk Wayne away from the house.

WAYNE: (yelling) "You can't let my ex-wife live in your house!"

OBED: "Then you take her."

Stu, Clare, and Grace go into the house and watch from the front window.

ADA: "Do you ever look at them, Wayne? Do you ever see your children?"

WAYNE: "Stay back, Ada."

ADA: "Do you ever see any of us?" (The pent up tension of church camp is boiling.)

For once, Ether lets me go.

CARTOON

The boys are watching *Heiffer and Rocko,* a television cartoon. Tubal, Noah, and Caleb watch it every morning, they say.

NOAH: "It's a machine that sucks."

TUBAL: "It sucks up everything." (He becomes the machine sucking his brother's arm.)

Raymond is with Wayne, trying to keep him out of Cora's way, trying to keep him from running, from breaking his extended probation.

Tubal continues to suck up his brothers. They scream and try to run.

ADA: "Tubal, turn off the machine."

TUBAL: "Schhhluuuulp." (It's a word that does not have letters to give it space.)

NOAH: "It's a cow and a wallaby. They have an apartment. It's their vacuum cleaner."

Noel and Nolie are both gone for the morning. Ether is at his office. I, alone, have the boys to myself.

THE OVERHANG

After church camp, Noel and Nolie work at Sparrow Hawk Camp in the summer. Wes leads canoe trips on the Illinois River. I know what they do because I hear them talk. Nohead Hollow. Molly Fields Cemetery. Ross Cemetery. Elephant Rock Park. Hanging Rock on the General Stand Waite Memorial Highway (Confederate Army).

One afternoon, Robert comes for Riley and George.

ADA: "You went to church looking for someone to take over your problems. For a while you stuck with it, when it was new. But you found that church was being a part of community, of giving. It's hard to go to church."

ROBERT: "Then why do you go?"

It is more than Robert and his wife can understand, or any of my brothers.

Now it's Nolie who doesn't want to go to church. I see it more and more. Each Sunday she takes longer to get ready, waits in the car after church is over while we talk to others.

ADA: "Has something happened?"

NOLIE: "I just don't like it. There's nobody to talk to. I don't know what they're talking about."

RILEY: "It's boring."

ETHER: "The book of Revelation is boring? The day of judgment?"
NOLIE: "Dad."
NOEL: "You find it to mean what you find it to."
ADA: "I'm not sure I like that answer either."
We stop on the dark road after a Sunday night service at church to look at the stars. We've got nearly all the cousins with us.
ADA: "What formed the aloneness?"
ETHER: "It's not lonely. You only see it that way."
NOLIE: "I see Mom waxing the floor of the stars."
NOEL: "The stars are married."
ADA: "A roller rink."
TUBAL: "Beaver teeth."
ADA: "A tree with stars for leaves."
NOEL: "The stars are gas stoves. The sky eats when it's dark. Their mothers get home in time to cook."
NOLIE: "It's a Sunday school lesson. Something I don't understand."
GRACE: "A thorn bush."
ADA: "Flurries."
WES: "Fish."
GEORGE: "A turtle crawling across the sky."
TUBAL: "Beaver teeth."
ETHER: "George is right. The sky's traveling outward."
NOLIE: "I didn't know this was a class."
ADA: "A keelboat."
CLARE: "Hail."
RILEY: "The night sky losing its way."
GRACE: "Buttons – I see Grandma sewing." (We return to the earth from the summer's night sky.)

NOLIE STARTS HER REPORT FOR HIGH SCHOOL

NOLIE: (when school starts again) "What did we do when we got here?"

ADA: "Where?"

NOLIE: "The Cherokee after Removal."

ADA: "The people built cabins, planted a row of corn, ate squirrels and rations. I suppose they were hungry sometimes."

NOLIE: (looking at one squirrel chasing another in the yard) "Why do they go on?"

ADA: "To go on."

NOLIE: "Litter after litter."

THE OTHER DUST BOWL

I start work at the library again. I look through an article for Nolie:

> In 1887, the U.S. government enacted the Dawes Severalty Act, which abolished the ownership of land, providing for surveying and allotment of land to Indians according to a formula:
>
> To each head of a family, one-quarter of a section (160 acres);
>
> To each single person, over eighteen years of age, one-eighth of a section (80 acres);
>
> To each orphan child under eighteen years of age, one-eighth of a section; and
>
> To each other single person under eighteen years, one-sixteenth of a section (40 acres).
>
> The unassigned land as well as 1.9 million acres purchased by the federal government from the Creek and Seminole tribes, in what is now central Oklahoma, was then declared open to white settlers, beginning at noon on April, 1889. On that appointed day, the U.S. Army held back thousands of eager settlers waiting at the border until a pistol shot signaled the start of the land rush. More than 50,000 settlers moved into the territory, and in a single day Oklahoma City and Guthrie each became cities of 10,000 people.
>
> By 1910, Indians were only about 175,000 in a state of more than 1.4 million. Within 20 years, two-thirds of the Cherokee lost their land allotments,

sometimes selling to white settlers, but often because they were unable to pay their taxes.

In 1891, Cherokee had owned 19.5 million acres in what eventually became Oklahoma (1907). By 1971, those holdings had dwindled to less than 150,000 acres.

But the prosperity of the Sooners proved to be short lived. The white homesteaders depleted the topsoil and cut down forests to provide timber for their cabins and fences. The erosion of the soil by wind and rain turned much of Oklahoma into the Dust Bowl.

RELOCATION

I sit in Manuscripts and Rare Books. No one needs my help at the moment. I open the cage door and look through the books. I read while standing at the shelves.

One time I went up there to Chicago where my brother lives. Rabbit is his name. He was right there when I got off the bus. We were a little hungry so we stopped to eat on the way across town. This restaurant we stopped at was all glass on the outside, like one big window. You could see all the people eating inside. They weren't sitting down either; they were all standing at the counter that wound all around the place. They were standing along both sides of this counter, but they didn't seem to be talking to each other or looking at each other. It was like they were all looking at the wall.

My brother and I decided to eat at a place called Wally's Bar over near where he lives at Fullerton and Green. There were a lot of people in that place and they were all friendly. They all seemed to know my brother too, but they called him *Indian Joe.* I hadn't ever heard him called that.

Rabbit told me he didn't have any place where I could stay. He had an apartment, but they'd had a fire there a few days before. We went over to look at it, and I guess he hadn't been there for a few days because there was a letter from Momma on the stairs right where you came in. There was black soot on the stairs all the way up to the fourth floor, where his apartment was; and there were some Puerto Rican guys up there cleaning the place up. They had the radio turned on real loud playing some kind of Puerto Rican music. The whole place smelled like charcoal and burnt furniture.

The story goes on to say that he didn't think he was ready to settle in Chicago and returned to the bus station and went back to Oklahoma.

The story, called "Relocation," also is in Cherokee.

ᏧᏂᏄᏬᏍᏓᏗᎢ ᏗᏂᏲᏎᎯ

ᏥᏔᎪ ᎠᏇᏅᏒ ᏦᏍᏓᏓᏅᏟ ᏗᎦᏁᏄᎢ. ᏥᏍᏚ ᏧᏙᎢᏓ ᎾᎿ
ᎡᏙᎲ ᏧᎴᏬᏍᏗ ᎠᏆᏑᏒ. ᏍᏗᎩᏓ ᏗᎦᏚᎲ ᏗᎦᎾᏗᏫᏒᎯ ᏭᎩᎾᎵᏍᏓᏴᏅ.
ᎯᎠᏃ ᏧᎾᎵᏍᏓᏴᏗ ᏂᎦᏓ ᎠᏓᎨᏗᏖ ᎨᏒ ᏙᏱᏗᎲ, ᎢᏧᏔᏖᏊ ᏌᏊ
ᎤᏔᎾ ᏦᏔᏂ. ᏂᎦᏓ ᏗᎪᏩᏛᏗ ᎨᏒ ᏴᏫ ᎠᎾᎵᏍᏓᏴᎲᏍᎬ ᎦᎵᏦᎦ
ᏗᎲ. Ꮭ ᎾᏍᏊ ᏊᎾᏂᏁᎢ. ᏂᎦᏓ ᎠᏂᏙᎾᎥᎢ ᎤᏥᏤᎦᏫᏓ ᎠᏊᏔᎾᏄᎢ.
ᏂᎦᏓ ᎠᏂᏙᎾᎥ ᎢᏧᏔ ᏗᎲ ᎠᏊᏔᎾᏄ, ᏝᏍᏊ ᏊᏂᏌᏂᏍᎨ ᎠᎴᏍᏊ Ꮭ
ᏱᏓᎾᏓᏫᏂᏍᎨᎢ. ᎠᏁᏍᏛᎢ ᏫᏓᏂᏫᏅᎢ.
ᏦᏍᏓᏓᏅᏟ ᏙᎩᏂᏚᎪᏓᏁᏄ Wally's Bar ᏚᏙᎠ ᏧᏪ-
ᏅᏒᎢ ᎾᎥᎢ Fullerton and Green ᏚᏙᎠ ᎦᎵᏅᏛ. ᎤᏂᏣᏘ
ᏄᎾᏛᏅ ᏴᏫ ᎾᎿᎢ ᏧᎾᎵᏍᏓᏴᏗᎢ ᎠᎴ ᎾᏍᏊ ᏂᎦᏓ ᎤᎾᏓᏅᏘ ᎨᏒᎩ.
ᏂᎦᏓ ᎬᏬᎵᎩ ᎢᏳᏍᏗ ᎨᏒᎩ ᏦᏍᏓᏓᏅᏟ, Indian Joe ᎠᏃᏎᎲᎩ.
ᏝᏃ ᎠᎩᏛᎦᏅ ᏱᎨᏎ ᎾᏍᎩ ᏄᏍᏛ ᏚᏙᎥᎢ.
ᏂᏍᏚ Ꮭ ᏄᏢ ᏳᏌᏢᏎ ᎠᎩᏒᏍᏗᎢ ᎠᏉᏎᏄᎩ. ᎤᏙᎵᏓ
ᎨᏒᎩ ᎤᏒᏍᏗᎢ ᎠᏎᏃ ᎤᎪᏁᏄᎩ ᎯᏄᏍᎩ ᏄᏒ ᏥᎨᏒᎩ ᏭᎩᏁᏅᏒ
ᏤᎩᏂᎪᎵᏰᎥᎢ, ᎠᎴᏍᏊ ᎯᏄᏍᎩ ᏄᏒ ᎬᏪᏙᏄ ᎨᏒᎩ. ᏭᎩᏂᏥ ᏅᏓ-
ᏳᏅᏁᏄᎯ ᎪᏪᎵ ᎦᏅᎩ ᎠᎩᏣᏩᏒᏍᏗᎢ ᎦᏣᎯᏍᏗᏳᏟ ᎾᎥᎢ. ᎤᏦᏄᏅᎯ
ᎠᏞᎲᎢ ᏗᏔᏏᏅᏍᏗᎢ ᏅᎩᏁ ᏗᏲᏓᏞᎲᎢ ᎾᎿ ᏳᏓᏅᎯᏓ ᎤᏒᏍᏗ ᏄᎵ-
ᏍᏔᏅᎢ. ᎠᏂᏍᏆᏂ ᎠᏂᏍᎦᏯ ᎠᏂᏅᎦᎵᏍᎬᎢ. ᏗᏬᏃᎩᏍᏗ ᏍᏓᏱᏳ
ᏧᏂᏍᏚᎢᏓ ᎨᏒᎩ. ᎠᏂᏍᏆᏂ ᏧᏂᏃᎩᏍᏗ ᏚᎾᏛᏓᏍᏛ. ᎤᏦᏄᏅ ᎠᎴ
ᎤᎪᏅᎢ ᎦᏬᏒᎬᎢ ᏂᎬ ᎦᎵᏦᎦ.

The Cherokee syllabary was made after the English language filled the land. I remember learning to write in English. (Cherokee was not taught when I was in school. Later I learned to write a little. Sometimes I write in Cherokee. Sometimes.) There was something solid in the process. The written words were something I could touch.

Syllabary	Pronunciation	Translation
ᎪᏪᎵ ᏗᎩᏁᏍᏗ	Go-(h)we:-li di-gi-ne:-s di______.	Written material it-I get-at ______.

PHOTO ALBUM

ADA: "Do you remember the tree that fell on our car?"

RAYMOND: "None of the trees in our yard fell."

ADA: "The tree at Grandpa's – we had to come back from Sallisaw on the bus."

RAYMOND: "I thought we rode in Grandpa's truck."

ADA: "That was another time – before we had a car."

RAYMOND: "It was the only black car Dad had."

Photographs are like books. Whole stories are carried in them. There is a way we look at books differently – interpret and remember them.

SHUBA: "Ada, your written words are sorcerers. They draw memory out of the head."

THE DREAM OF MY MOTHER SOMEWHERE

There is a land. It is green. There is another land beyond it. Someone was beheaded in the night. The head became a planet in orbit. Someone in a long robe holds a book, its metal face closed with a snake or a small lightning bolt. The land is bottle green. Do not think I have forgotten.

It's an old story of the powers of the air. It's where some of our dreams travel. Our head leaving our body. Sometimes we see the spirits in our dreams, or we get indirect images of them. The dark powers don't want us to know about them. Yes, they want us to believe them, because then we're afraid, and they work their magic against us. But if we don't believe, we laugh and walk straight into them as though they weren't there. But sometimes (maybe it is their arrogance), they let themselves be seen. Then we've seen them, or part of them; we know they are there. We know they like to intimidate with terror.

ADA: (to Ether the next morning) "I think the dream was telling me that Mother got through to the other world. I didn't see her struggling against the air."

Ether reads the newspaper. He doesn't like to hear about the dark powers, though in physics, I tell him, there's plenty of it – the fusion – the changeableness of elements – the distortions – the one thing becoming another – the unknown – all of it is also witchery and sorcery from the dark spirits.

It's in the night the dark spirits come from the next world. I hear them knocking on the roof. Just as I wake, they stop, but the knocking is caught in that rim of waking, that margin between awarenesses of both worlds.

A spell works in conjunction with belief. The giving and receiving. Spoken intent combined with receivership.

I saw a spirit once. A dark spirit. It had radiant hair and eyes in its elbows. When it flew, sparks trailed its feet. Raymond was with me. I think it was Raymond. We were walking down the road from our parents' house when the spirit flew above us. It must have been on the road and we startled it. It was doing something and hadn't seen us coming. We stood there with our mouths open in awe of the living being not of our world. Then it flew away. It was a magical transformation.

The dark spirits can make chickens talk. They can make someone fall and get hurt. They can make things happen. That's why I'm a Christian. It is the only thing stronger. Belief in Christianity. Belief and practice. A combination of units. It is the same in the power of the dark world, which was once a part of the light but pulled away because it wanted itself more than the light.

We used to think we knew who the witches were. There was an old woman who had several dogs. We called her *tsi:sgili.* Witch. We'd walk down the road, spy on her, and run back. Maybe the dark spirit Raymond and I saw was coming from her place. You want to watch them, but you can't; you have to back away or you begin to feel a part of them. That magnetic pull gets a hold of you. That electricity that lights you up and you have to have more – more and more of it – then there's no stopping you. You become one of them, or a possession of one of them. You begin to work spells on others. You become a *spoiler of the sacred.* You don't spoil God. No, God goes on as he always does; you don't soil him, but you spoil him in others, those who would believe, who would become Christian. You spoil the whole kingdom of God for them.

A witch violates families. Sometimes Mother thought a witch had our family. She would have the church pray for us. Just look at our family torn up since the beginning. What have we done? Why can't my brothers be at peace with themselves? That's the mark of the work of the witch. We've all seen witches. All of us. Robert. Wayne. Raymond. I've heard Robert say that on the road at night, sometimes the trucks with their lights are like eyes of dark spirits as they drive through the night. Sometimes he feels possessed by the momentum of the road. This process in motion. This moving while in motion. That's witches for you. Riding the air. They are manifestations of the dark world. They aren't just one force, but multiple. They run many ways at once. That's their hidden power. All the witch's tools – thorns, animal hair, slivers of bone – can be shot through the air and somehow cause disease.

THE HEAD LIBRARY

The head librarian visited the New York City Library on a trip. *The granite building covered two city blocks,* she said, *the stone lions on each side of the front steps. The library of libraries.*

There were rooms of books in long rows, some behind glass doors. There were Periodical Rooms. Map Rooms. History Rooms. Rooms of drawers and old card files. Research Rooms. Exhibition Rooms. Special Collections Rooms. Meeting Rooms. There was the Astor Reading Room for Rare Books and Manuscripts. The Microform Room. The Trustees Room.

There were prints. Lithographies. Photographs. Murals. Further books.

There were sky lights. Marble floors. Wood paneling. Staircases. Long corridors.

THE LIBRARIAN: "They have original manuscripts – the Guttenberg Bible, Jefferson's manuscript of the Declaration of Independence."

She took out a New York City library card. A library card from the New York City Public Library.

ADA: (to myself) "As though she'd be back to return any book she borrowed."

THE LIBRARIAN: "Outside: The pigeons. The traffic. The noise."

THE DUST BOWL (2)

In the roller rink that used to be a roadhouse that used to be a meeting house that used to be an encampment. They are here. It's just that our here is their there. It is sometimes the relationship of where and here that interchanges. But it is there in the here where they are.

I watch the dotted air moving in the roller rink. Skating is like passing along the river's edge under the sun/shade through the overhanging trees.

I see the spirits spin in circles of light. *Chuka chu.* The words skate. I love the rolling language.

The spirits pass through this world, stop for gas. Do they see us, and we see them without knowing? Do some of them come to the library to read about the newer world? I have looked down on the first floor at the students reading. Who is real and who is a spirit dressed in jeans?

Some of the spirits roller-skate. I almost know who they are.

I think through the genealogy:

Raymond, my brother (Tubal, Noah, Caleb, his sons, (named by my father))

Wayne, my brother (Stu, his son)

Robert, my brother (George, his son)

Obed, my father (Robert, Wayne, Raymond, his sons)

Reuban, my grandfather (Obed, his son)

Saban, my great-grandfather (Reuban, his son)

To-we-sah, my great-great-grandfather (Saban, his son)

No-we-tah, my great-great-great-grandfather (To-we-sah, his son)

No-no-tah, my great-great-great-great-grandfather (No-we-tah, his son)

They move between worlds.

Skaters in the rink of sorrow who saw their world change.

Robert, Wayne, and Raymond still kicking against the loss. What used to be. What would come out of them? My brothers, their sons, the progeny of men who knew their way home, I say to Wayne, Raymond, and Robert, who can't yet move between worlds.

I felt tears at the flash of recognition, at the importance of both worlds rushing together around the rink (as do oral and written words).

The tears that came one after another like clay pigeons out of the skeet shoot we used to go to when I was a girl. In the blackgreen bottlefly car (before the tree fell on it).

There was the dichotomy. The two skating rinks. I understood. For just a moment, I understood.

CREATION MYTHS FOR THE WRITTEN WORD

The Maker sells aluminum siding. He bends many nails installing it, which the people pick up to use for letters of the alphabet. As long as the Maker sells his siding, there will be plenty of letters.

The alphabet is like a flock of birds feeding in a field, but the Maker sneezes and the birds startle into the air with possibilities of differing combinations.

Once a Buick drove up, emptied its ashtrays: the butts were the first letters of the alphabet.

At one time the Maker collected insects, but his net fell open and the insects swarmed out across the field in different directions.

A long time ago, the voice was lonely. The Maker looked for a rib. That's why the alphabet is the bones of the voice.

Once a spaceship landed, swept out the black bits of space caught in the grille: those particles of space dust were the first letters of the alphabet.

The voice kept telling stories, faster and faster, louder, louder, until the voice caught fire. After the blaze (which raged for days, some say) (or months, according to others), people touched the ashes with their fingers and made the first written words. Now stories can be told without combustion.

At one time, language was invisible; it could only be heard, but it got in the way of a spray painter.

THE DREAM (6)

My fingers are bloated. I look and they are oars. I am a boat. The river stands still. It is the rocks in the river that are moving forward, the water giving them resistance. I look and see the clouds are standing still; it is the sky moving toward them, covering them with its blue again. I am pushing the river with the oars that are my hands, saying, *come on now, it's all right, you can move again.*

All day my fingers row.

Somewhere in the night I look at the sky.

The stars are rowing.

No.

The stars are moving as if written letters of an alphabet.

DESIGNS OF THE NIGHT SKY

Yes. The stars are alphabet. That's where the idea for writing came from: the stars. They are written words; their constellations moving the way books in the library circulate. Written words are the lesser lights. Yes. The greater light is still the sun, the voice.

I have a line of students to direct to different manuscripts and old books. I am in the middle of understanding something and I have to help them. I want to let go of them all, but I know the structure that holds. I have decided to hold onto it.

Rabah calls about Riley. What time did she leave our house last night? Ether was tutoring her. Wes, Noel, and Nolie were teaching her to make fry bread for Indian tacos, which we had for supper. There were so many, Wes's parents ate with us. There were so many, we called Obed, Cora, Grace, Clare, and Stu. I don't tell Rabah that Riley stopped several times for phone calls. If Rabah wants to know about Riley, she should ask Riley's cousins to make a mess in her kitchen. She should have the stink of rolling grease in her house. Why is it always Ether and I who go through school again and again?

Day unto day utters speech, and night unto night shows knowledge. There is no speech nor language, where their voice is not heard (Psalm 19:2–3).

That is what I want to understand. There is no language where the voices of the day and night are not heard? Language comes from the air? The sky and heavens, the atmosphere, the above-the-earth, the stars! Once you're inside the Bible, it's like being in the cage of Manuscripts and Rare Books. Locked! The old voices open. You roll all over the place.

Their line is gone out through all the earth, and their words to the end of the world. In them has he set a tent for the sun (Psalm 19:4). Yes, the language of the upper spheres holds our lives. Words are made of air, but their written form is like the stars seen from the earth.

A star fell to the earth – the people picked up the broken parts, and they became the first written words.

I show the students where to find the words they need for their papers and reports. Those words are what they need to pull them through – I don't tell them – but show them – those words pull you along.

I think sometimes Riley hears.

Some of the students return to ask for more help. Would they like me to write their papers for them? Can't they think what to do for themselves? I want to take a stick to them, but the words from the sky give me a distant sense of release and I answer what they ask.

An assistant professor is at my desk.

ASSISTANT PROFESSOR: "Are there any articles on why writing is important?"

I can't think of any.

ASSISTANT PROFESSOR: "The students question why they need to write papers. I thought maybe someone had explained it in an essay."

ADA: "This is Manuscripts and Rare Books. You might want to ask downstairs. I know there are old stories about the importance of stories. We don't know who we are without them. I know that writing refines our cognitive abilities. It clarifies our thought processes. It shows us how far we have to go."

ASSISTANT PROFESSOR: "Students think they can get along without it."

ADA: "Yes, sometimes I feel their resentment when they have to research papers."

As I talk to him, I remember other verses in the Bible. I know the stars will fall. I know *the stars will withdraw their shining* (Joel 3:15).

Maybe that's how it will happen. The students will refuse to write. They will live in their computers. They will live online. They will forget the former way of communicating.

Maybe it's the written language that desires to leave the earth and return to the sky.

There are other verses I think about: *The stars are not pure in his* (God's) *sight* (Job 25:5). Maybe written language is not the final version. Maybe it has to undergo rebirth, transformation, or translation also. Our corrupted and corruptible language.

I will share that with the Truthettes on Saturday.

But for now we have written words, those birds that fly, those stars that fall.

THE VOICES

Library books are made of trees. Therefore, a library is shade.

It is democracy itself (different voices side by side). Voices from the Old World conjuring. Voices from the Christian evangelists. All speaking together, seemingly from the same place, woven into a braid of voices, but coming from separate places.

I drive south to Sallisaw, Oklahoma, for a meeting of librarians. We eat at Lessley's Café (since 1947) near a plot of flowers planted in the shape of Oklahoma.

We meet in the old train station, which is now a library, the Stanley Tubb Library, on Oak and Cherokee Streets in Sallisaw.

My family is from northeastern Oklahoma. They lived in several log cabins from Tahlequah down to Sallisaw. There was something about Little Vian Creek. A field of wild yellow flowers. The names of Oklahoma towns: Waleetka, Okfuskee, Wetumka, Okemah, Wewoka, Watonga.

Ho. Inside the library: the sweet, the inconsolable voices. The words. The little friends.

SEQUOYAH'S CABIN

A liveliness is lost in the writing down.

Foe, J. M. Coetzee

He alone is left to do the thinking. How will he keep them all in his head, all the books, all the people, all the stories? And if he does not remember them, who will?

Boyhood, Scenes from Provincial Life, J. M. Coetzee

Sequoyah invented the Cherokee syllabary in 1821. His old cabin, maintained by the State Historical Society, is eleven miles north of Sallisaw.

On my way back to Tahlequah, I stop by the cemetery where my grandparents are buried. Then I decide to stop at Sequoyah's cabin.

A cedar cabin chinked with clay remains in Oklahoma, preserved by another house over it, built by the State Historical Society. To see Sequoyah's cabin, I first must enter the house built over it, then enter his: a table, three-legged chair, fireplace, and narrow ladder to the loft beds. Perhaps it is symbolic to enter what is seen and find a smaller duplicate inside, where he once stood with book and pipe, in robe and buckskin, leaning on his cane, a turban around his head like an artichoke. He made a written language from recurring sounds so we could reach another from that place within a place. It was at that table he sat and pulled the prickly leaves of Cherokee speech so we could find within a sound a language to relate, a written word that has a meaning: a house within a house. The pungent wood-pulp smell of artichoke fills the cedar cabin where Sequoyah worked for years making a character for each word but the characters became too many like the words of someone trying to be understood. Then Sequoyah made a character for each sound he heard, inventing characters and using English letters, which he did not know. He spoke only Cherokee, spoke only from the language of the heart. He combined the characters for the sounds he heard (from his window within a window, his house within a house). Then he stood at the table, the three-legged chair, in robe and buckskin, smoking his pipe, the alphabet on a parchment under his arm so we can work within ourselves, pulling artichokes from the heart.

NOEL STARTS HER FIRST REPORT FOR COLLEGE

When I get back to Tahlequah, Noel is at the table writing a paper for history. I look over her shoulder at the notes she has made:

Cherokee a southeastern tribe

DeSoto's exploring party encounter 1540

Controlled large parts of the Carolinas, Virginia, Tennessee, Georgia and Alabama

Over 60 towns

dwellings a pole framework covered with woven mats plastered over the clay

towns largely independent, ruled by a chief, a council, and a war chief

divided by seven matriarchal clans

Smallpox 1720

Noel covers her notes with her hands as I read.

ADA: "I want to see what you write."

NOEL: "This is my report."

I go to the kitchen, where Wes is reading.

Nolie has started supper.

ADA: "Where's your father?"

NOLIE: "Upstairs grading papers at his desk."

On my way upstairs, I stop at Noel's notes again:

Cherokee hunted with blowguns and bows / arrows
farmers / corn, squash and sweet potatoes
Shamans used chants / spells cured and inflicted injuries

I hear Noel sigh.

She reads from the book (frowning because I am still there).

NOEL: "The Cherokee learned rapidly from the Europeans. By the end of the eighteenth century, despite population loss to smallpox, they had become farmers, some (a few) had plantations and were slaveholders.

Recognizing the importance of European writing, Sequoyah devised a syllabary/written language for his native speech. By 1821, the Cherokee translated hymns and the book of John. They published a newspaper, the *Phoenix*."

ADA: "Noel, you won't believe this, but I stopped at Sequoyah's cabin on my way back from Sallisaw this afternoon."

Noel ignores what I say.

NOLIE: (from the kitchen) "Is that why you weren't here to start supper?"

NOEL: "In 1827, the Cherokee established themselves in a republic, printing in their own language a constitution modeled on the United States Constitution."

I watch Noel make more notes:

President Andrew Jackson dispossesses the Cherokee west of the Mississippi even though Supreme Court declared dispossession illegal
Removal 1838 (splitting the tribe in two because some fled and escaped the boat trip (and march) / some stayed in the southeast)

NOLIE: "Now don't you wish you were at the University of Oklahoma in NORMAN, HUNDREDS of miles from HERE?"

WES: "It isn't that far."

I continue to read Noel's notes:

Forced to migrate on foot

(and keelboat, Noel adds)

to Arkansas / Missouri / finally Indian Territory (now Oklahoma). Though factionally divided, they nevertheless gradually established themselves – despite allotment / loss of sovereign status

ADA: "Noel, you're copying out of a book. Why didn't you use your own words?"

Noel snaps the book shut.

I get the picture.

ADA: "Why are we the only ones here? Why don't we have cousins running through the house? Jumping off the roof? Rearranging the trees?"

THE SPELL

Cora and my father wake in the night. They hear a *rigging,* Cora later calls it.

ETHER: "A what?"

OBED: "Something that *rigged.*"

There are a series of strange nights. Sounds. Stumpings.

ADA: "What's up?"

RABAH: "It's meant to scare Cora out of your father's house."

ADA: "Spells?"

RABAH: "If you think so."

Cora stays at my father's house. Grace, Clare, and Stu want to stay there too.

ADA: "Who would do that? Shuba is the conjurer."

ETHER: "You can't say that."

ADA: (to Cora) "Do you want to stay with us?"

CORA: "You don't have room."

The house continues to *rig.*

INDENTATION

Obed Nonoter's house is on wheels! Skates? Can that be? Both he and Cora, and Grace, Clare, and Stu, say the house moves. They are in their beds at night. Cora between Grace and Clare. Stu in a large closet in the hall. Obed's room is on the front of the house. He says the trees go by. No. The trees are still. It's the house that moves. He knows it.

CORA: "A spell. What else can it be?"

I know she suspects Shuba. I do too. But in the Truthettes, we feel Christian forgiveness and let go of our suspicions.

Shuba says she is not putting a spell on Obed's house, though she and Raymond would like to help Wayne, who wants Cora out of his father's house.

Shuba says again she knows of no spell. But Clare finds a spell nailed to the house.

CORA: "Look at that writing! Shuba *is* putting a spell on the house so Clare, Grace, and Stu will go with Wayne."

ADA: "Wayne can't take care of himself, Cora. I don't think he wants to take the children away from you."

Ether looks at the spell. *Nitched,* he says.

I look at the spell: *to cause someone to move*

tobacco to remake to smoke it, one
early morning remake

(Blow smoke toward the house of the one you want out. Repeat four days. The person will get the feeling he is not wanted there.)

Look at the writing of the spell. Is it not from the night sky too? The written words are a power field also, the same as the voice, going out in many ways.

I look at the written spell again. I see the writing is marked.

ADA: "You left the Note, Raymond! It's your handwriting! I've seen it before. I recognize those curls and notches in your letters."

RAYMOND: "Wayne dented my van."

ADA: "He's your brother."

SHUBA: "He has to pay for the repairs."

INDENTION

Learning to write in school: move the first line over: indent.

Why?

It lets the reader know there's another paragraph.

Why?

You can't have different parts of the story – different thoughts – lumped together.

Why?

Because they have to be separated.

Why?

Sit there 'til you learn to indent.

Indent (from *dentis* or *tooth*) (v.) To cut a toothlike point, to notch, to space in from the margin (to make new paragraphs).

Indentation (n.) A slight hollow (where what ______ is left out?).

Indention (n.) A blank space left by this.

Without paragraphs, would we have indention?

Without paragraphs, could Wayne file for bankruptcy? (Which he is.) Could his girlfriend leave a note that she is tired of him (and run off with someone else)?

Indention is the blank space where Raymond leaves his senses and casts spells.

Robert's indention is when he's on the road.

Riley's indention is her absence from Robert's house.

George's indention is his cruelty to animals.

Rabah's indention is that she won't see what's going on.

I could go through them all.

And mine ______ mine?

WAYNE: "The spell's on me. I feel it."

ADA: "I heard the lawyer's words in court, Wayne. They're keeping you out of jail so you can work. You've got children. There's construction work available. They'll garnish your wages to pay child support."

Wayne is agitated.

ADA: "Even Cora pleaded for you. It sounds like mercy to me."

WAYNE: "I feel like I got a headband around my chest." (He butts his head against the courthouse door as we leave.) "It's airtight in a conjurer's spell."

ADA: "You've done damage to the boy's family – the boy's bicycle – Raymond's van – Cora, Grace, Clare, Stu – all of us. I think it's guilt you're feeling."

WAYNE: "There's no way out. It's a foggy night. I can't see the road."

ADA: "It's all the bad decisions you've made. The bad behavior."

WAYNE: "It's a black coffin of a spell."

ADA: "You're blaming everyone but yourself."

WAYNE: "There's a cloud around me."

ADA: "Come out of it, then. You can walk through a cloud. Spells have no power unless you believe they do. Belief is the magic of a spell."

WAYNE: "You holy rollers have your own spells. But conjurers' spells are worse."

ADA: "No, Wayne."

WAYNE: "Wait 'til you hear Shuba say, *I'll send my leopards after you.* Just wait 'til you hear that."

ADA: "I chose the anecdote to spells. I'm not afraid, Wayne. *He set my feet on a rock and established my goings* (Psalm 40). It's written in the Word. I don't walk into spells."

We stop at Wayne's beat-up, dust-covered truck with the license plate hanging crooked. I see the padlock open on his toolbox.

ADA: "The Word is my shield and fortress."

WAYNE: "I'm in a pit. I feel the swimming blackness in bed at night."

ADA: "If I walked in that sloggy stream, I'd retrieve my foot. Close off the possibility of spells."

WAYNE: (getting in his truck) "You ain't seen the leopards."

ADA: "Lock up your tools, Wayne. That way the witches won't get them."

Wayne drives off in his truck.

LOCATION

Ether talks to Nolie about her church attendance (or lack of it) at supper.

ETHER: "Faith is – the strings of physics."

STU: "Strings?"

ADA: "Faith is something that always will be there for you, Nolie – like leaves."

Noel looks at her plate (probably wishing she'd gone to the University of Oklahoma in Norman). Wes has an eye on the television in the other room (though he can't hear the sound). Nolie is telling Stu he should eat his green beans (so she doesn't have to give her full attention to us) (Stu is not listening, but watches Wes watching television)).

I listen to Ether (so he knows someone is listening).

ETHER: (grateful for Stu's inquiry) "The basic unit of matter is strings – energized matter that vibrates in different ways – and causes everything that happens."

ADA: "I don't know that I understand."

NOEL: "No one has seen the strings, but mathematical formulas tell us they are there."

ETHER: "They are tubes of energy – so small we haven't been able to see them yet."

WES: "Energy that has form."

Nolie is listening to Ether now because he has forgotten he is supposed to be talking to her about going to church. If she keeps listening, he will keep talking about physics.

WES: "– pockets of energy – loops –" (Wes is helping Nolie without even knowing it).

STU: "– that are stringy."

Wes pats Stu on the head.

ADA: "That's what language is. Surely the spoken word. Maybe also the written – different versions (or loops) of stories. Stories next to stories, overlapping borders. We use parts of them to tell again in our own way – long conversations of different stories."

Ether is looking at me.

Noel sees Stu putting green beans in his pocket so he doesn't have to eat them.

NOEL: "Get them out, Stu, put 'em on your plate. You still have to eat them."

Stu pulls one out and looks at it.

ADA: "It's linty, Noel. He can't eat them."

NOEL: "Pass the bowl, Wes. I'll put more on his plate – some clean ones."

Stu looks at Wes.

WES: "I can't do that to my pal."

ADA: "Get them out of your pocket, Stu."

NOEL: "What a father you're going to be someday."

Stu cleans out his pocket. The beans are covered with lint and ravelings and dirt. Wes puts one green bean from the bowl on Stu's plate and one on his.

WES: "I'll eat mine if you'll eat yours."

Nolie gets up from the table and takes the dishes to the kitchen. It is her turn to clean up. Wes and Stu drift toward the television. Noel decides to help Nolie.

INTERMEDIARIES

The books have voices. I hear them in Manuscripts and Rare Books, where I work. Sometimes I dream the voices as I read. I go to that place where book *is:* A c(or)r(al) for story (a place where oral tradition is *penned*). There is a road through a field and I walk through it. There are yellow flowers in the field. It is evening. The sun is behind the low clouds. The clouds move as slowly as turning pages in a book. Usually the road is bleached in the hot sun. But the rain turned it brown. Thunder overhead shakes the road. Sometimes lightning zips across the sky as if it were on roller skates. I am part of the old ones as I walk. I am part of the ones who will come. *I will turn to the people a new language* (Zephaniah 3:9). A spoken word. A written.